NO CREAM PUFFS

NO CREAM PUFFS

Karen Day

WENDY
LAMB
BOOKS

Published by Wendy Lamb Books
an imprint of Random House Children's Books
a division of Random House, Inc.
New York

Visit us on the Web! www.randomhouse.com/kids

Educators and librarians, for a variety of teaching tools,
visit us at www.randomhouse.com/teachers

Library of Congress Cataloging-in-Publication Data
Day, Karen.
No cream puffs / Karen Day. — 1st ed.
p. cm.
Summary: In 1980, when twelve-year-old Madison, who loves to play baseball,
decides to play in her town's baseball league, she never envisions the uproar
it causes when she becomes the first girl to join.
ISBN 978-0-375-83775-3 (hardcover) — ISBN 978-0-375-93775-0 (Gibraltar lib. bdg.)
[1. Baseball—Fiction. 2. Sex role—Fiction. 3. Friendship—Fiction.
4. Michigan—History—20th century—Fiction.] I. Title.
PZ7.D3316No 2008
[Fic]—dc22
2007030018

The text of this book is set in 11-point Goudy.

Book design by Trish Parcell Watts

Printed in the United States of America

10 9 8 7 6 5 4 3 2 1

For my parents, Jim and Nancy

And for Billie Jean King

1

This isn't what we usually do.

If we have time after lunch, we shoot baskets with the boys in the gym. Today we're lined up in front of the mirror in the girls' bathroom.

I stand to the side and twist my mood ring around and around my finger. My mess of curly blond hair is a disaster compared to the new feathered style everyone else has. "This is Plushy Pink." Casey Cunningham pulls a tube of lip gloss out of her purse and opens it. The sweet smell of cotton candy fills the bathroom. She rolls it onto her lips. "It's new."

She rolls it onto Gina's lips and then reaches for Sara, who stands next to me, holding her new purse with both hands. I'm next.

Casey snaps the cap on the lip gloss and puts it back in her purse. I feel the tops of my ears burn; she left me out on purpose. I glance at Sara, but she won't look at me.

"You smell like a circus," I blurt. Their lips sparkle under the lights. Could my lips look like that, too?

"I'm sorry, Madison." Casey looks at me, eyes wide. "I didn't think baseball players wore lip gloss."

I glare at Sara, who drops her eyes. She promised not to tell anyone. She knows I'm kind of scared, what a big deal this might be. It's 1980. Here in Michigan girls don't play league baseball with the boys.

Sara and I have been best friends since second grade, and this is the very first time she's ever told a secret of mine. How could she?

"Are you really going to sign up?" Gina asks. "Be the only girl?"

Everyone looks at me except Sara. She turns the stone on her matching mood ring around into her palm so I can't see the color. *We'll never take them off,* she said to me last fall when we bought them at the mall. Is there a color for guilt?

"I don't know." What do they think about this? What should I say?

"I wouldn't know the first thing about playing baseball," Casey says.

I watch how she leans into Sara and puts her hand on Gina's arm. Casey's nose is tiny, her eyes big and brown. She's so cute, and you just want to be with her, be singled out by her. That's how I felt, anyway, until I realized how mean she is.

Sara's cheeks are pink. Still she won't look at me.

What to do? Get out.

I run into the hall and into the cafeteria. I stand against the wall, breathing in and out, and stare at my feet. I'm wearing what we always wear, Tretorn tennis shoes, stained with dirt, full of holes, shredded at the tongue. No socks. Jeans and a T-shirt. Today Sara showed up in sandals and carrying a purse.

When I hear voices, I look up. Billy Evans sits with the other sixth-grade boys at a nearby table. He's pointing at me, snickering. I glare back. Is he making fun of me again?

One day last week Billy and I were the final two playing Horse in the gym. Everyone was watching and I'd just sunk a ten-foot jump shot when the bell rang. He still had time for one last shot, but he turned to go.

"Come on, Billy, we can finish this." I wanted to win. Billy and I were just about even, and it was fun playing against him.

"Chicken!" a boy on the sideline yelled at him. Everybody laughed.

Billy looked at the boys. Then he pointed at my chest. "How can you play with your boobs in the way?"

Everyone was silent. I looked down at my T-shirt and saw how my breasts poked out. I wanted to melt into the gym floor.

They all started snickering. I ran from the gym.

Now I watch Billy's big mouth move up and down, and heat rises up through my back and into my head. What if he says something about my chest again?

"Shut up, Billy, you big jerk!" I yell so loudly that kids turn to look.

"*What?*" Now he's in front of me. He's the only boy in sixth grade as tall as me, and we glare, eye to eye.

"You heard me!" Billy *is* a jerk and everyone knows it.

"So what are you gonna do about it, tomboy?"

"Don't call me that!" My heart is pounding; people crowd around us. Out of the corner of my eye I see Sara, Gina and Casey.

"You gonna beat me up?" He pushes closer.

"Shut up!"

Everyone laughs. Billy turns and smirks at his friends.

My head grows hotter. Before I know what I'm doing, I punch him, my fist catching the side of his cheekbone. My fingers throb as if they've been slammed in a car door. I look at Sara and the girls.

Then I fall backward. When I hit the floor, it all catches up with me. Billy has punched me, and my nose and cheek explode in stinging, hot pain, worse than my hand. I burst into tears.

Billy stands over me, his fists raised. Then he drops his arms. Something warm flows over my lips and chin.

"Gross!" Casey says.

I wipe my palm across my face. Blood covers my hand; I lick it off my lips and stand. My head throbs and I see little white bursts all around me. I have to get out of here. I turn to my friends.

Sara's mouth hangs open. Casey pulls her arm and Sara hesitates but then takes a step back with the others. I feel as if I've been hit again, this time much harder. Is Sara going to just *leave* me here? *Abandon me?* How could she? This is way worse than telling Casey about baseball.

This is way worse than anything she could ever, ever do!

"Thanks a lot, *Sara.*" I take off my mood ring and throw it at her.

Then a cold, wet towel is shoved under my nose and my head is pushed forward. Someone holds my arm and leads me away. I twist my head to see Mrs. Post, my gym teacher and volleyball coach.

She guides me around the corner and into her office. I crawl onto her couch and turn over.

"Let's take a look." She lifts the blood-soaked towel off my nose. "For God's sake, Madison, what were you doing fighting with him?"

"He's such a jerk." Everyone watched me hit Billy and saw how much harder and faster his fist came back. I shouldn't have looked away. Is everyone laughing now? This will spread like crazy through school.

"I don't think your nose is broken." Mrs. Post sighs. "But this is completely unacceptable, Madison. A boy shouldn't hit a girl, *ever*, no matter what!"

I nod, then stop. Does she mean that a boy shouldn't hit a girl but a girl can hit a boy? That doesn't seem right.

"You're lucky I was the lunch monitor. I wouldn't want my star volleyball player to end up in the principal's office."

She sighs again and smiles. I relax. Mrs. Post is great. She's young and wears sneakers and T-shirts. She can be spastic and silly. Like the time Sara and I danced on her desk after volleyball practice. Instead of getting angry, Mrs. Post climbed up to dance with us.

"*However,*" she says, "I should find out what happened to Billy. I guess you can't get suspended, since this is the last day of school. Stay here. No goofing around. You don't want your nose to start bleeding again."

My *star volleyball player.* I smile. Last fall our team went undefeated. Even though I had the most kills and the most points on my serve, she's never called me a star before.

The season was *so* much fun. Sara, Gina, the girls and Mrs. Post. It was our first time playing volleyball and I picked it up easily.

Now I squeeze my eyes shut. Sara told me last week that she might not play next year. And Gina's already decided she won't.

I know why. Casey Cunningham doesn't think it's cool. And Casey doesn't think I'm cool, either.

I sit up. My hand and nose are still throbbing. Will I have a black eye? At least I wore a dark shirt that doesn't show the blood. All my T-shirts are too tight now, and it would have been awful lying on the floor, blood all over my chest. I glance at the clock. One more hour until school is over for the summer.

When I hear Mrs. Post's voice in the hall, I lie back down. I put the towel across my nose and eyes, dried blood facing outward.

"Oh, dear, dear, *dear.*" It's Mrs. Campbell, our principal.

"I don't think it's broken." Mrs. Post lifts the towel.

I moan. I want her to think I'm in too much pain to go back to class.

"Maybe we should call her mom, get her to the hospital," Mrs. Campbell says.

My eyes shoot open. "I'm okay. I just need to rest." And not see anyone. Ever.

"She can stay here," Mrs. Post says. "I'm just packing up."

"Well, all right," Mrs. Campbell says. "But what were you thinking, Madison? Fighting with a boy. And he hit you in the face! He could have really hurt you."

"I'm sorry." I'd do anything to undo what happened. And I'd say anything to get her to leave.

"Think about this. It's not ladylike to fight with boys. Violence is no way to solve a dispute. Ever. I'm going to talk to Billy now." Then Mrs. Campbell turns and leaves.

My luck has changed. No punishment. No suspension. No school until next fall. And time with Mrs. Post. I sit up and watch her stuff gym suits into cardboard boxes.

"Let me help." I jump off the couch.

"No. You need to rest, remember?" The phone rings and she answers it.

I see Mrs. Campbell's face in my mind and something tightens in my chest. What is being ladylike, anyway? What you wear? What you do? What you like? I pick up a bat and begin swinging in slow motion.

The tape on the handle is worn away, but the wood is smooth. When I play with my brother, David, and his friends, I always use David's bat. It's heavy, but I usually hit just fine. This bat is better, the right size.

I swing again and when I turn Mrs. Post is off the

7

phone, watching me. "My brother wants me to sign up for the town league," I say.

She nods. "Are you going to do it?"

"I don't know. I'd be the first girl. What would you do?"

She laughs. "Well, I may be a coach, but I was never the kind of athlete you are. *That's* for sure."

I frown. I wished she'd said she was just like me. Or I'm just like her. But she's right; she's not that great at throwing or batting. She's better at telling us what to do.

"You're certainly good enough, better than most boys," she says. "I'd love to see you play. You'd have to figure out how to deal with the pressure."

She smiles. I smile back even though I'm thinking. Pressure because I'll be the only girl? Or because baseball is hard?

David told me that the official Little League began accepting girls in 1974. But our league isn't part of that. It's small, run by the parks department, and there are no rules about whether girls can play or not.

I squeeze the bat handle. There are no baseball or softball leagues for girls in our little town. Girls play volleyball and basketball during the school year. The only team sport for girls over the summer will be a week of volleyball camp, run by Mrs. Post.

Maybe baseball would be fun.

When the bell rings I wait a few minutes before saying goodbye. The halls are empty as I pull everything out of my locker: notebooks, candy wrappers, socks and dozens and dozens of notes from Sara and the other girls.

I sit on the floor and open one of Sara's notes. *Madison, wait for me at your locker after gym class. I really NEED to TELL you something! BFF, Sara.*

I remember that day. Sara told me something hysterical that Gina had said in English class. We laughed so loudly that everyone in the hall turned to look at us.

I feel an ache as I fold up the note. Sara introduced me to Gina on the first day of school. Gina had gone to a different elementary school, but she and Sara knew each other at their country club.

Gina was funny and friendly and by the second day we had a group of seven who sat together at lunch, slept over at each other's houses on weekends and went together to the boys' football and basketball games. Four of us played volleyball.

Sara was still my best friend. But I loved being part of a big group. Laughing. Riding bikes. Talking about school. This year was the best year ever.

Until Casey Cunningham moved across town to our school a couple of months ago.

I stuff everything into my backpack. Outside, I unlock my bike and take off.

The air is warm as it blows against my cheeks. I dodge cars and run stoplights. When I climb the hill near bus stop 22, I feel the air cool. Now I'm on Lake Shore Drive with Lake Michigan spread out below me.

I turn off Lake Shore Drive and onto my street and coast down the hill. Then I squeeze my brakes and nearly fly over the handlebars. My mom stands in the driveway, talking with some of the neighborhood moms.

It's way too early. She should still be at work.

I can tell by the way she pulls her shoulders back and frowns that Mrs. Campbell called her. I'm in trouble. As I inch down the hill my nose and cheek begin to throb again.

2

Mom and the neighbors turn as I stop, not too close to them. I straddle my bike and bring up my hand to hide my face.

"Mom?"

"Let's go inside," she says. "We have a lot to talk about."

I sit on a stool in the kitchen as Mom leans across the counter. She rarely wears makeup and today the circles under her eyes are darker than normal. She looks at me and I have to resist touching my nose and my cheek.

"Your nose looks very sore," she says.

"It was unbearable. I was in *agony*." I lower my eyes.

She straightens and sweeps her hand across the counter,

making a pile of toast crumbs and Cheerios. "When I got out of court today, I had a message from your principal. She said you were in a fistfight?"

I stare at the counter. I don't want to think about Billy or Sara or any of this.

"You hit a boy? And he hit you? In the face? What in the world were you both thinking?"

"I don't know."

"Well, you must know. She said you hit him first."

I open my mouth to tell her about the girls in the bathroom and how Billy keeps making fun of my breasts. I don't know why, but I can't tell her.

"He's just a jerk, Mom, and everyone knows it."

"But why did you hit him?" She leans across the counter again until her face is level with mine. From outside the screen door I hear the voices of the Tulliver kids playing in the sand dune behind the houses.

I close my eyes. I hit Billy hard, but his fist came back so much harder. And all that blood. And then my friends backed up and just *left* me there.

The screen door opens and David walks in, his face red and sweaty. He's home early from caddying at the golf course. He opens the milk, sniffs it and pours a glass. "So, Maddie, what's the verdict about the league?"

How can he think about baseball at a time like this?

Mom straightens. "Maybe I should call Mrs. Campbell so she can help me understand."

"What's going on?" David asks.

"Never mind." The last thing I want is for David to get in the middle of this.

"What? Detention again for passing notes?" He laughs.

"Shut up."

"That's enough," Mom says.

David sits at the table and opens the newspaper. I glare at him. He's such a know-it-all. Just because he's sixteen. Just because he never, ever gets in trouble. Well, *I'm a better baseball player than you are!* I'd never say this, though, because he'd feel as lousy as I do. "Mrs. Post thinks I should sign up for the league."

David glances at me. He wears his brown hair short and little drops of sweat cling to the hairs above his ears.

"You *should.* I told you that." He gives me a longer look. "What happened to your face?"

I glance at Mom. "I got in a fight with Billy Evans."

"And he *hit* you?"

"Yeah, but I hit him first."

David whistles. "I can't believe he hit you. I bet you embarrassed the crap out of him. Did everyone see it?"

I scowl. When David puts down the newspaper I snatch it off the table and hold it up, hiding my face. I stare at a picture of the U.S. Embassy in Iran.

Then I pretend to be all interested in an article about the hostages. This is what I know about it. Some Iranian students took these Americans captive at the embassy. They want us to return the Shah, the King of Iran. I don't know why America has their shah, or why the Iranians want him back. This is one of those things David and Mom talk a lot about, but I hardly ever pay attention.

The phone rings, and I peek over the top of the paper as

13

Mom picks it up. "Hey! I tried to call you earlier. How's everything in Milwaukee?"

It's Susan, Mom's college roommate. They sometimes talk for hours. I've been saved!

Mom walks to the refrigerator, the phone tucked between her chin and shoulder. She pulls out a head of lettuce and picks off the brown leaves at the sink. Then she reaches for a law book on the counter, opens it and reads something to Susan while she continues to pull the lettuce apart.

How does she do all these things at once?

"Your mom is so smart," Susan said to me one day. But I already knew that. Mom's friends always call asking for lawyering advice. I don't think she ever loses a case.

Mom laughs and says, "Uummmm." She drops the lettuce into a bowl.

But she can be so confusing. A woman should be able to support her family, she tells us. Yet instead of working for a law firm that would pay more money, she works as a lawyer for the town for hardly anything. We're pretty broke.

She wears flowing skirts and gauzy blouses and sometimes goes out of the house with a pencil stuck in her hair. But she's always talking about taking personal responsibility and doing your best. She's never on time for anything, she hardly ever cooks a real dinner and last week she almost forgot my parent-teacher conference. But she says being a mom is the best job in the world. Now she isn't even punishing me.

I tip back on the stool and feel my nose. It barely hurts anymore.

After dinner I sit on the porch and use my toe to dig into the sand until I have a big enough hole for my foot. Most of the front and back yards of the houses on our street are like this, full of sand and dirt and patches of scrubby grass. Behind the backyard, the sand dune climbs nearly two stories high.

Rex, the Tullivers' Labrador, walks up our driveway and nuzzles his nose into my thigh. I scratch under his collar the way he likes it.

I kiss his nose and watch him run off after a squirrel. I sigh. After what happened today, I don't think I'll be talking to my friends anytime soon. What will I do all summer? Volleyball camp isn't until August.

Mom told me once that Gina was a "fair-weather friend." But *Sara?*

Sure, we've had lots of fights. In fourth grade our teacher chose Sara to push Annie Kendall around in a wheelchair when Annie broke her leg. Sara acted as if it were the most important job in the world, ignoring me as she pushed Annie through the halls. I didn't talk to Sara for a week.

But then she got pretty fed up with Annie bossing her around, and things went back to normal.

This is different. How could she tell Casey about baseball? How could she leave me in the cafeteria?

I hold up my hand and wiggle my bare finger. Two days after we bought our mood rings I lost my booklet explaining what each color meant. So every night on the phone Sara explained my mood to me.

"I'm the same as always, boring green," she said the other night. "You're dark blue again? Oh! That means you're happy, romantic, passionate and going to fall madly in love."

But I've never felt very romantic. And I sure don't know who I'll fall in love with.

I go grab my baseball glove and start throwing a tennis ball at the garage door, aiming at a small square David drew with a piece of chalk. I begin counting the pitches that land in the square. One, two, three. Then all the way to twenty-five.

I didn't think baseball players wore lip gloss, Casey said.

Why can't I do both? Not once did I think this might be a problem. But maybe everyone will laugh if I pull out a tube in front of them, and watch to see if I put it on right. What if I don't have the right color? The right kind?

Last Saturday I opened a tube at the pharmacy and rolled the tip over the back of my hand. It was clear with little red sparkles and smelled like cherries.

Lip gloss and clothes were never that important to Sara and me. But after Casey arrived, Gina started dressing like her. Nice hair, matching socks and shirts, earrings, lip gloss. And last month Sara came to school with her curls blow-dried straight and pierced ears.

I wind up and pitch. The ball hits the center of the square and bounces back to me. When I turn, I see my mom. She's still in her work clothes—a flowered blouse and yellow skirt. She's barefoot, her long, curly blond hair pulled back with a rubber band. She sits on the porch and pats a space next to her. I sit.

I can tell she wants to talk about today. So I say the first thing that comes to my mind. "Did Dad ever pitch?"

She stiffens. "No. He played third base."

"But he was a good hitter, right?" I already know this. A couple of years ago David wrote to the athletic department at the University of Wisconsin and they sent Dad's playing stats. He started at third all four years he played.

Mom nods. "What makes you ask?"

I shrug. We don't talk about Dad that much. But ever since David brought up the league several weeks ago, I've been staring at the picture of Dad on my bureau. What would he think about me playing baseball?

I haven't seen him since I was five, when Mom got a divorce. She was tired of living on army bases all over the world, following a husband who was gone on missions for months at a time, once even for a year. Her dad, Gramps, had died and she missed her mom here in Long Beach. She wanted to do "something" with her life. So we moved here.

The truth is, I only know a little bit about my dad. He never made an error at third base. He loves Wisconsin. And he loves the army, because that's the main reason Mom said she left him. He didn't have room in his heart for anything other than his job.

"I wonder where he is." I think about the picture of the embassy in the newspaper and sit up. "Do you think he's in Iran, trying to save the hostages?"

"I don't know."

"But he could be. He could be over there right now,

working on another plan to get everybody out." She frowns, and I scrunch my shoulders up and sigh. Just get to the punishment.

"Oh, honey, I wish he were here for you." She puts her arm around me and pulls me close. I nudge my head into that familiar part of her neck, where the skin is warm and sticky. She smells faintly like lemons and an awful lot like the onions she cooked tonight.

I pull away so the neighbors won't see me sitting so close to her. And that alien voice in my head is back, criticizing everything she does. *Why do you always answer questions with more questions? Why don't you pluck your eyebrows?* These things didn't use to bother me.

"But he's busy, right?" I say. "You said his job takes him away for months."

"True. But Madison, you know his job isn't the reason why he hasn't been in contact with us. With you."

I scoot away, bring my knees to my chest and hug them. Then I let go and slip my hand into my baseball glove. The leather is cool and soft.

"What happened today, Madison? Why were you fighting? Mrs. Campbell said Billy Evans was teasing you. What did he say? I want to know. Can we talk about this?"

I roll my eyes and look away. The streetlight in front of Mrs. Minor's house blinks on. I stare at it until my eyes blur.

She sighs. "You could have gotten *really* hurt. I can't believe he hit you. And so hard." She reaches over but I pull away.

"Everyone laughed." And Sara, Gina and Casey left me.

This hurts so much that I can barely breathe, but I don't know why I can't tell her this.

"Laughed at what?" When I don't answer, she continues. "Ignore them. Find another way to fight back that doesn't involve punches. Think of something creative to say. Violence is not a way to solve problems."

Creative? I never know what to say!

"When it's just you, alone and against the odds, you have to pull out that special thing, unique to you, that will enable you to stand up for yourself."

I roll my eyes. Here we go again. Mom is always telling us *I was the only woman on law review in law school.* I dig my fist into the pocket of my glove.

"Well." She smoothes out her skirt. "You cannot fight like that. Someone could get seriously hurt. So, as punishment, you'll have to stick around the house for the next couple of weeks. No beach. No friends' houses. You can stay here with Mimi."

Mimi's her mom, my grandma. She's great. But . . .

I should just tell Mom what happened. Then I think of last winter in the department store when we went to get my first bra. She said right in front of the clerk, *Honey, it's so wonderful your breasts are making themselves known!*

She thinks things like bras and getting your period are the greatest things that can ever happen. She'd be so disappointed in me if she knew I hit Billy because of what he said. But what kind of special, creative thing was I supposed to pull out to answer *that*?

"What about the town league?" I say. Change the subject.

"Do you want to play?"

"Do you think I should?" I glance at her.

"Only you can make that decision."

I punch the pocket in my glove. Can't she be more helpful about stuff like this?

3

Three nights later I stretch across my bed, my chin resting on Gertrude, my Raggedy Ann doll. I've spent the day with Mimi, planting green bean and tomato plants, and my knees are sore from kneeling in the dirt. Yesterday we cleaned the basement.

Every summer since we moved back here Mimi's stayed with David and me while Mom works. But usually I'm all over town on my bike or playing baseball with David and his friends. It's going to be a long couple of weeks if I have to hang around the house all day.

I glance at Dad's picture on my bureau. His blond hair sticks out from under his Wisconsin baseball cap. Mom told me this photo was taken right after they met, and I like to think his grin is because he's so excited about her.

Sometimes when I'm eating breakfast I pretend I hear a voice and I turn to see him standing at the screen door. Or when I'm pitching to the garage door I imagine he's standing there, telling me what to do. Or maybe we write letters back and forth, telling all about our lives. And he's funny and interested and knows everything about sports.

I don't remember much about him. Mom said he was "indifferent" and didn't care one way or the other if we stayed or went. But I've always wanted to believe that if he'd gotten to know me, or if he knew me now, he'd like me. He'd want to stick around.

I go to my window and push out the screen, climb through the opening and onto the roof. It's quiet in the neighborhood and still light. I like to come out here and look at the stars, see what the neighbors are up to. When the wind is right I can hear the waves on the lake.

From here I see the entire street. Some neighbors, like Mrs. Minor, are old and live alone. Others, like the Fraziers and the Jenningses, have little kids. No one my age lives on the street. Which has never been a big deal because my friends aren't far away.

Three days and no one has called.

Then I hear angry voices below. I scoot across the roof to see a stranger standing on Mrs. Minor's lawn. He wears leather hip-huggers and no shirt, and his blond hair hangs on his shoulders. Mrs. Minor is wearing her lime-green housecoat, and she glares at him from just inside her garage.

A thrill races up my back. The stranger is breaking the golden rule on our street. Never, ever mess with Mrs. Minor's lawn. Even Rex knows enough not to pee on it.

What a huge mistake!

"Oh, come on, lady, smile," the stranger says.

I need to get closer. I scoot farther down and brace my legs against the gutter. Maybe he's Mrs. Minor's long-lost son. Maybe she's been searching for him for the last twenty years and now that he's finally home she's mad at him.

But didn't Mom tell me that Mrs. Minor never had any children?

He takes a breath as if he's about to say something, then shrugs. He walks across her yard, disappears into Crystal Adams's house on the other side and slams the screen door behind him.

Then a voice says, "What are you doing up there?"

I gasp, my foot slips and I fall off the roof and into David standing below me. We both sprawl on the ground.

"God, Madison." He stands and brushes pine needles off his shorts. "You could have killed yourself. Mom would have a fit if she knew you were up there again."

"I know. I'm sorry."

"Do you want a matching black eye?"

I touch my nose, where a faint blue and green bruise stretches to the bottom of my eye. Still tender. "Who was that?"

David takes off his cap and scratches his head. "I think he's Huey Milligan."

"Huey Milligan, the singer? No way." Huey Milligan is famous. "What would he be doing in Crystal's house?"

"I don't know. I came outside to go run and there he was, arguing."

"What about?"

"Mrs. Minor wanted to know who he was and why he was in the house, since Crystal was at work. He told her who he was, but she hadn't heard of him."

Huey Milligan! His old song "Ain't Done Fightin'" was the theme song for my sixth-grade class this year. I used to see him on the news on TV—there was a concert when he smashed his guitar, and once he was hospitalized after jumping off a hotel balcony into a pool. I haven't heard anything about him in a long time.

Is this real? I glance across the yard to the redbrick house where Crystal lives alone. "How long will he be here?"

"How should I know?" David bends over, stretching his legs.

"How does he know Crystal?"

"Madison, I don't know. . . . Doesn't Crystal work at some club near Notre Dame? Maybe Huey was playing there."

I nod. During the day Crystal works at Hinton's Grocery store. On weekend nights, at a club in South Bend. Maybe she snuck backstage. Maybe she did something crazy again. I know a secret about her. Crystal is a complete maniac.

"I wonder what he's doing here," I say.

"Oh, no, you stay away from him." David shakes his head.

"I'm going to meet him."

"Right. He'll probably be gone by tomorrow. Besides, he's old. What would he want to talk to you about?"

"I can think of some things."

"Nothing you could say would interest him, Maddie."

I can tell him to be careful of the dangerous riptides in the lake. I can tell him that Mount Baldy, down the road, is one of the biggest sand dunes on the Great Lakes. And I want to ask him: Why did you smash your guitar? Have you been to Germany, where I was born? Why are you with Crystal? What's it like to be famous?

Until today, Johnny Phillips, the state tennis champ, was the most famous person in Long Beach. But Huey Milligan is world-famous. Or he used to be.

But I can't just walk up and ring the doorbell and say hello.

Can I?

"Well, I'm not going to go over there right now."

"Good." David bends down, stretching again. "Don't go over there at all."

I shrug. David takes off running down the driveway and I go inside. I sit in my window watching Crystal's house. Nothing happens.

After an hour I go downstairs, where Mom is in the living room, her papers and notebooks spread across the couch. She doesn't look up when I open the front door. Outside, the air is humid and warm and mosquitoes buzz. David sits on the steps, sweat dripping from his chin, his running shoes and sweaty socks next to him.

"I caddied today for John Weeks," he says. "You know, the gym teacher at the high school. He coaches in the league. He said he'll take you on his team. I bet he's a good coach, Maddie."

I step into the yard and look at Crystal's house. Only the light above the front stoop is on.

It might be nice to do something while I'm grounded. And it's just baseball. Who cares if I'm the first girl to play?

But I can imagine what Casey will say if I sign up.

I touch my nose; it feels okay. How will the girls even know if I play? Hardly anyone goes to league games. It won't be that big of a deal. What else am I going to do this summer?

David tosses a sock at me. "It's a short season, Mad. Only six or seven games. Just try it out. The first practice is tomorrow. I'm going up to Warren Dunes with Artie and D.J. but not until two. I'll take you."

"Okay." I look at Crystal's house. Nothing has changed, but I feel as if things are looking up. I'll go to practice. Then afterward I'll pay Huey Milligan a visit.

The next morning I slide my hand into David's glove and look at his name; he wrote it on the leather with a marker. It's a big deal that he let me borrow his glove. Last winter he saved all his snow-shoveling money to buy it in time for high school baseball tryouts in the spring.

I glance at him as he drives. He's short and thin, like Mom. Mimi says he hasn't come into his body yet. He wears a red baseball cap with a big white W on the front. After he was cut from the high school baseball team, he was asked to be the manager. Mimi says it takes a special person to be able to do that after such a big disappointment.

I pick at the scrape on my knee that I got from falling off the roof. I *did* see Huey Milligan last night. Right? It seems unreal today. Huey is a legend, "a rock-and-roll icon whose future is less secure than his past." That's what the article said about him in an old *Rolling Stone* magazine I read on microfiche earlier this morning at the library.

At breakfast I said to Mom, "I should probably read a lot of books while I'm grounded."

She was so happy to hear I was going to do something "constructive" with my time that she took me to the library right that minute. When she went upstairs to read the newspapers, a librarian helped me find the article and ran off a copy for me to bring home.

I'm going to keep Huey a secret. I don't want anyone else trying to get to know him.

David turns off Lake Shore Drive, and I watch Lake Michigan disappear behind me. My heart takes a giant leap as we near the junior high school.

"Who else is playing?"

"Don't worry. Once everyone sees what you can do, it'll be okay."

"I'm not worried." I touch my cheek, where the bruise is fading.

David taught me to play years ago, when he and his friends played every day in the field behind the Phillipses' house. At first all they needed was a catcher. But then I moved over to first base and for the last two summers I pitched. Baseball seemed pretty easy. Nobody cared that I was the youngest and the only girl.

"A lot of towns in the Midwest have already gone

through this. At first it's a big deal for a girl to play. It'll die down, especially when everyone sees how good you are."

"What will die down?"

David parks and opens his door. "Come on."

I get out and follow him. A dozen boys stand talking on the field. It seems as if every single one of them has a dad nearby.

The boys go very quiet as they stare at me.

I recognize two from school. The rest must go to other schools. All the teams are made up of ten-, eleven- and twelve-year-olds. I hope none of them have heard about my fight with Billy Evans.

My eyes stop on a boy with big blue eyes and hair so blond it's white. He keeps throwing a ball into his glove. When he smiles at the boy next to him, I feel a tingle race through my legs. He's just about the cutest boy I've ever seen.

Maybe this is a good idea after all.

David introduces me to Mr. Weeks. Several of the dads smile. When I look at the boys, most drop their eyes. *Hey,* I want to shout, *look at me.* We form a circle around Mr. Weeks.

"We had a great team last year, and we can have an even better team this year," Mr. Weeks says. "So let's have fun."

"And win," says a boy with red hair. He frowns at me.

My back stiffens.

"Games are once a week. All positions are open," Mr. Weeks goes on.

I'm glad he didn't say anything about me joining the

team. He hands out uniforms and then motions for me to follow. We stop at the girls' restroom on the other side of the bleachers. "I thought you'd like to try on your uniform in here."

I should tell him that I haven't made up my mind. I rub my finger on the bill of the new red cap. Might as well try everything on.

Inside, I slip on the uniform and stare in the mirror. HINTON'S, the name of the team's sponsor, runs across the front of my shirt in red letters. No matter how hard I tug at the shirt, my left breast refuses to go anywhere but in the middle of the *o*. It's as if someone has drawn a red target around it. When I pull on my cap, my blond curls shoot out on both sides of my head. All I need is a red ball on my nose and I'll be Bozo the Clown.

What would Sara think? Casey? I never used to worry about things like this. Or if I was pretty or needed lip gloss or a purse. I try to swallow the lump in my throat. Then I hear voices coming through the vent by the sink.

"Let's just give her a chance. After that, if you don't like it, you don't have to play." A dad's voice floats through from the boys' bathroom.

I slump against the sink. So many people are laughing at me lately.

I close my eyes. And for some reason all I see is the square David drew on the garage door. It's easy, really easy, to pitch to that square. Not just once in a while. A lot. And all in a row, even when it's dark and the only light I have is from my mom's reading lamp, which shines through the family room window.

I take off my uniform and hand it to David, who waits outside the door. I slip on his glove and run to the field.

This is a real baseball diamond, with a backstop, team benches and bases. Not like the field behind the Phillipses' house. There I know the ground rules. A triple if you hit the oak tree in left field. A double if you hit the shed on the first-base line. A home run if you hit over it. I lick my lips and shift my feet.

Some of the boys play catch, while others take batting practice. I decide to wait at the plate behind the redhead and the cute one.

The boy in the batter's box is little and skinny, with shorts that hang past his knees. He keeps swinging late and missing. Finally he hits a foul down the first-base line. He smacks his bat on home plate and then hoists it back on his shoulder. The bat is almost as big as he is. Is there a lighter one he could use?

"Choke up, Donny," Mr. Weeks says as he throws the next pitch. The boy scoots his hands up the bat but still keeps missing. "Next time use the black bat. It's lighter."

The cute boy's name is Tommy. He's tall and tan. What would it feel like to touch his arms? His skin looks so smooth.

"What kind of a name is Madison?" the redhead asks.

"Just a name." I'm used to people asking.

"It's like Wisconsin. Your parents named you after a town in Wisconsin."

"You're right."

"Really? That's weird. I'm going to call you Wisconsin."

"I don't care."

Several boys laugh. I dig the tip of my bat into the dirt.

"So, Wisconsin, what position do you play?" He smirks. The boys laugh again.

What's so funny? I take a deep breath. Think of something creative to say. "I pitch."

"We already have a pitcher." He points across the field, where a tall boy with curly brown hair winds up and throws to a dad. But he's too far away for me to see how well he pitches.

"Randy's probably going to go pro someday," the redhead says. "He can already throw a curveball. Can you throw a curve?"

I shrug. All last summer I begged David to teach me how to throw a curve. "You're too young," he said. "You'll throw your arm out."

"But, Brett, we need another pitcher," a boy says.

Brett ignores him. "I catch, Tommy plays second, Doug plays shortstop and Brian plays first."

What about third? Besides, Mr. Weeks told us all positions are open. But I know what Brett is saying. No room for me. I shift my feet and glance at the boys. They all stare at me, except Tommy. So far he has yet to look at me. Is he even listening?

"I guess that leaves third base." I've never played third. Fielding is the weakest part of my game.

It's Brett's turn at bat. I watch him smack line drives to center field. He's a scrappy hitter and connects with every ball Mr. Weeks throws. I'm next. I put on a batting helmet and take practice swings. My arms feel loose and warm.

Just before I step into the batter's box, Randy jogs across

the infield and stands behind the plate. He's tall and skinny with huge feet and arms that seem too long for his body. Tommy whispers something to him and Randy nods. They're friends.

"Hey, Randy," Brett calls from behind the backstop, where he's putting on his catching gear. "Wisconsin says she's a pitcher."

"Who?"

Brett points to me and Randy shrugs. But there's something about the way he looks at me, eyes narrowed, lip turned up slightly, that reminds me of Billy Evans. I glance at my chest.

When it's my turn, I'm so nervous that I swing and miss the first pitch.

Brett laughs. "Way to go, Wisconsin." A couple of boys snort.

I step out of the box and take a practice swing. My dad had a solid .345 average when he played for Wisconsin. I imagine him standing next to me, telling me to lean into the pitch. Swing level. Keep my eyes on the ball. I get back in the box. My heartbeat slows and the next pitch seems to float toward me in slow motion.

I smack it deep into left field. The third pitch I hit over the chain-link fence and into the church parking lot. Then I start placing hits—down the right-field line, down the left-field line. When Mr. Weeks throws harder, I come around the ball earlier. I love the cracking sound the ball makes against the bat. How clean and sure my hits are.

When I've hit about twenty pitches, I turn from the box. The boys playing catch along the fence have stopped

to watch. A few of them smile. Brett comes out from behind the backstop, his mouth open.

Later, after Doug and Brian have tried pitching, it's my
turn. Randy, Tommy and the others stand at the fence and
watch. Brett crouches behind the plate. I tuck the curls
behind my ears, wind up and throw as hard as I can. Brett
sits in the dirt after he catches it.

Someone says, "All right, Madison."

Brett brushes the dirt off his shorts and walks to the
mound. I cross my arms.

"Do you always pitch like that?" he asks.

"I guess."

"Do you always hit like that?"

"Yeah."

"How did you get so good?"

"I don't know."

Brett kisses the ball and puts it in my glove. Then he
grabs me around the waist and starts jumping up and
down. "We're going to win! We're going to win!"

I burst out laughing. Then I glance at the fence. Randy
glares at me, but I don't care. For the first time in a week, I
feel as if I belong somewhere.

4

Later, I wait until Mimi is asleep on the couch, then walk up the dune in the backyard and cut across until I'm behind Crystal's house. I climb under the branches of the huge pine tree in the Adamses' backyard, where Sara and I used to make forts.

I part the branches and look out, but I don't see Huey. This is just the kind of thing Sara would love to do. She'd wait here with me all day for a glimpse of Huey.

I move the branches again. Huey's in the window! His hair is pulled into a ponytail and a cigarette dangles from his lips. What's he doing in there with Crystal? She's only twenty-two, a lot younger than he is, but I suppose they could be boyfriend and girlfriend. She's pretty, I guess. But she never talks to anyone. What would he want with her?

Huey turns from the window and disappears.

After a few minutes Crystal pulls out of the garage in the big blue Oldsmobile her dad left behind when he moved to Ohio. I run out from under the branches and along the side of her house to see her drive away, her head just above the dashboard.

I know that look, the way her eyes droop, her lips slightly parted. I've hardly ever seen this expression change, not even at her mom's funeral three years ago. When Crystal walked out of the funeral home, her face was the same as when she rings up my mom's groceries every week.

I walk into Crystal's backyard, where patches of grass stand shin deep and weeds sprout in the sandy parts.

I rise on my tiptoes to the kitchen window and look in. Beer and pop bottles line the counter next to an empty Bonnie Bakery bread bag. The sink is filled with dirty plates and glasses. Two red roses float in a cereal bowl filled with water.

I walk up the concrete step to the door and look through the screen. What does Huey do all day? Write songs? Practice his guitar? Has he smashed up anything in the house? Maybe he was kicked out of his hotel for jumping off the balcony again.

But this is so exciting, having someone hugely famous like Huey Milligan staying here. Nothing like this ever happens in Long Beach. And no one knows except Crystal, David and me.

I lick the sweat off my upper lip and knock.

I'm about to leave when Huey finally comes to the door.

He stands in his leather pants and an unbuttoned long-sleeved shirt. He doesn't even say hello.

We stare at each other. I can't think of a thing to say.

"Who are you?" His voice is softer than I imagined, as if he just woke. I thought he might scream instead of talk. That's how his singing sounds.

"A neighbor."

"Oh, well, hello, neighbor." He smiles.

I smile back. Huey opens the door and steps onto the stoop. The hair along his temples is gray and his skin is the color of our beige couch. But he doesn't seem that old. Maybe that's because of the way he stands, hands in his pockets, shoulders drooped. Or how big and friendly his eyes are. He smiles again.

"You should know one of the rules of the neighborhood," I say. "Never walk across Mrs. Minor's lawn. She sods it. It's very expensive."

Huey looks across the yard. The sun has gone behind the sand dune but Mrs. Minor's lawn still sparkles. "How do you sod a lawn?"

"Well, you get some people to bring in a big truck with this grass that's rolled up like a carpet. Then you unroll it on the dirt, and presto. Instant lawn."

"Well, thanks for telling me," he says. "I won't make *that* mistake again."

"Sure." I usually don't talk this much to adults, especially ones I don't even know. But he doesn't seem like an adult. And he sure doesn't seem like a big rock star, either. Is he as old as my mom, my dad?

Huey sits on the stoop and looks up at me, squinting. A

ripple of excitement shoots through me. I'm here with *the* Huey Milligan!

"Who are you?" he asks again.

"Madison, the neighbor. I live on the other side of Mrs. Minor."

What's he doing here? He could date *anyone*. I wonder if he knows that Crystal's a maniac; that once she wandered around in a snowstorm wearing only a summer nightgown. And doesn't he wonder why she's living alone in this house with the weeds and sand? No family. No friends.

Huey yawns, stretches out his arms and rubs his bare feet in the sand. I slowly lower myself and sit next to him. "Aren't you hot in those clothes?"

"What? Oh, yeah."

He takes off his shirt. Something stings in my cheeks, but I don't look away.

"Where do you suppose I could get some decent clothes in this rinky-dink town?" He straightens and throws his long hair behind him. "In California we've got groovy stores on every corner."

It's not very polite that he's staying in Crystal's house yet bad-mouthing the town. This is something Mimi would have a fit over. The article about him in *Rolling Stone*, which I read five times this morning, talked about his humble background, his grass roots, the working-class neighborhood where he grew up.

"Yeah, but did they have groovy stores in Brockton, Massachusetts?"

His shoulders slump forward and his hair spills onto his

chest. He lets out a sigh. "How do you know about that?" His voice is soft again.

"Oh, I know everything about you! I know about your dad who's a plumber and your brother who's in jail. And the time you jumped off the balcony and the Gibson guitar people who were going to sue you for smashing your guitar.

"Even though 'Ain't Done Fightin' is really old, it was our sixth-grade theme song this year and Sara Cavanaugh and I made up a dance on roller skates to it and won runner-up in the school talent show. *Gone Fishin'* could have been one of the great albums of the sixties if you hadn't messed up the last two songs."

I feel a little pinch inside my chest when I say Sara's name. But this isn't the time to start worrying about all that.

"Messed up the last two songs?"

"You know, with that organ thing." I can't believe I'm saying all this to him. But he doesn't seem to mind. He nods slightly.

"You're still pretty famous." Even though he doesn't play in front of thousands of people anymore. But I don't want to hurt his feelings so I don't say this.

Huey glances at me. "Where did you hear all that stuff?"

"A *Rolling Stone* article."

"You didn't really believe all that, did you?"

"You mean your dad isn't a plumber?"

"No, I'm not talking about that. The other stuff."

The other stuff?

"Look. Fame isn't all it's cracked up to be. People always

want a part of you. Or they try to take you down. And these reporters, they meet you one time and think they know you. What's in your soul. They make judgments about you."

"Aren't reporters supposed to write the truth?"

Huey laughs the way David does when he wants to bug me. "What's truth? What does that mean? How can anyone really know *your* truth? Then, of course, you start believing what people write about you. . . ." His voice trails off.

"Huh?"

He rubs his hands down the legs of his pants but his palms stick to the leather.

"My brother is almost your size and there are plenty of places he gets clothes," I say.

"What did you say your name is again?"

"Madison. The neighbor." How come he can't remember this?

"Okay, Madison the neighbor. My clothes went back to L.A. with the band. Think you could let me borrow some of your brother's clothes till I can get new ones?"

I sit up. "Sure!"

I glance across Mrs. Minor's yard. Mimi will be awake soon. I stand. "Gotta go. I'll be back later with the clothes."

I sprint home. Now I have an excuse to go back and see him.

5

I lift my spoon but stop. David and Mom are talking about the hostages in Iran. The other day their discussion turned into a big argument and when I asked a simple question—has anyone seen my glove?—they both yelled at me. So now I just listen.

"All I'm saying is that we look weak, Mom, we do," David says.

"It shouldn't matter what we look like. We should do what's right and honorable. During the Vietnam War we secretly bombed Cambodia but lied about it because we worried what the world would think. We should have worried about what we were doing to the poor people who lived there."

I try to remember where Cambodia is. I look at David.

He's cradling his coffee cup in both hands and bouncing his leg.

"But we're a superpower," he says. "And we've let this little country push America around. What if they kill the hostages?"

"They won't kill the hostages."

"They might!"

"Look, David, I really respect that you're trying to understand this. But you tend to see things only from one perspective. *Your* perspective."

"No, I don't."

She nods. "You do. And this is a terribly complicated situation."

"But Mom, look at what the newspapers are saying!"

I tilt my head to get a better look at the paper. *You can't always believe what you read,* Huey said. Are there journalists in Tehran looking for truth and not finding it? Are any of them making bad judgments? ·

Last night I reread the article about Huey in *Rolling Stone.* I looked for judgments. Toward the end of the article the writer wondered if Huey's "juvenile and irrelevant lyrics mimic the man."

I suppose you can't get much more judgmental than that.

The spoon slips from my hand, hits the side of the bowl and tips it over. Cereal and milk spill across the table and onto the newspaper. I rush for a dish towel.

"God, Madison, watch what you're doing." David lifts the paper.

"It was an accident." I soak up the milk and carry the

rag to the sink. That was the last of the milk. How will I eat my cereal?

"You never pay attention to what you're doing."

"I do so."

"You just go at things a million miles an hour."

"No, I don't!"

"That's enough," Mom says.

David and I scowl at each other. I reach to twist my mood ring and feel a little pinch in my heart when I touch my bare finger.

David stands and puts his cup in the sink. I watch him move around the kitchen, folding newspapers, lifting the trash bag out from under the sink. He thinks he knows everything. Just once I'd like to see him forget his chores or mess up on his homework or not know the answer to something.

Mom watches David, too. She's dressed in an old flowered skirt and tank top. No makeup. How much better she'd look if she just covered the mole next to her nose. Or plucked her eyebrows. They're so bushy!

But when she looks at me and starts to speak, I turn away.

Mimi opens the door and comes in. She sets a grocery bag on the counter and pulls out a gallon of milk. "Thought you might need this."

"Thanks, I couldn't get to the store last night," Mom says.

I kiss Mimi. Her short hair is wavy and gray. She has a dimple in her cheek like Mom. Today she wears shiny red lipstick and smells like baby powder and soap. Her house, just a mile down the beach, smells like that, too. Fresh. Clean. And sweet.

When we were younger and Mom had to work late, David and I got off the school bus at Mimi's house. We sat at her kitchen table, dunking warm chocolate chip oatmeal cookies into milk while we did our homework. Mimi sat with us, reading the newspaper, and then, when we finished working, telling stories about Gramps.

Mimi runs her finger along the side of my nose and up to my eye, where the bruise has turned a yellowish green. She pats my cheek and smiles.

That afternoon I arrive at practice just as Randy and Brett head out to the field. I stand at the fence and watch.

Randy walks with his long arms swinging at his side, his feet scuffing the dirt as if they're so big he can barely lift them. He trips over the rubber, frowns and mumbles as he glances at me. I try not to smile. This is our team's best pitcher?

My smile fades once he starts throwing. His motion is smooth and he brings his arm up and over, unlike most boys our age, who bend their elbows to the side. Then the whole right side of his body follows his arm. It's perfect.

But the ball sails over Brett's head and into the backstop.

"Ready for a curve?" Randy says loudly, glancing at me.

"Just get it over the plate," Brett says.

Randy winds up and throws. The ball is high, then

drops wide to the left of the plate. Brett dives into the dirt to stop it. This time Randy doesn't look at me.

I watch him pitch. He's very fast, but if I were him, I'd slow it down and concentrate on getting it over the plate. Still, if he ever gets control, it will be hard to hit one of his pitches.

Mr. Weeks sends me out to the mound to take Randy's place, and Randy drops the ball into my glove without looking at me.

I throw easily, to warm up my arm. Then I throw harder and work the ball around the plate. My arm feels steady and strong as I bring it up and over my body. David taught me to pitch. His own pitching motion is awkward—kind of sidearm. But he's great at explaining what to do.

Smack. Another strike. Today I feel as if my body will do whatever I tell it out here. Follow through with your right leg, I think, and my leg does it. Sometimes my body does it automatically, as if I were born playing baseball. The same thing happened last year when I started playing volleyball.

After a while, Mr. Weeks walks out to the mound. Brett meets us. Mr. Weeks is tall, with brown eyes and hair speckled with gray. He's probably the same age as my dad. If Dad were here, maybe they'd like coaching together. "How does your arm feel?"

"Great." I take off my cap and my curls spring off my head as I wipe my face on my sleeve. My arm is warm and humming.

"She's pitching great," Brett says. "She always catches the plate."

Mr. Weeks rubs his chin. I glance over his shoulder at Tommy, who leans against the fence talking to Randy. Tommy's white shirt almost matches his white hair.

"You have a great fastball and you're really consistent, which is important," Mr. Weeks says. "How would you feel about starting in our first game?"

I look at Brett. But he just nods.

"Okay." I smile. Mr. Weeks said I have a great fastball!

"Let's see how you do against a batter." He jogs off the field and Brett goes back to the plate. A short boy with black hair puts on a helmet and stands in the batter's box. The helmet is too big, and the boy has to tilt back his head to see out from under the bill.

I start throwing, and the boy swings and misses every pitch. When he finally hits one, it dribbles halfway up the first-base line. I throw a dozen pitches to the next batter. He swings and misses every pitch, too. Finally, he swings wildly and hits a foul ball behind the backstop.

When Tommy steps into the box, I wrap my fingers around the seams and throw as hard as I can. He swings, misses, and the ball explodes in Brett's mitt.

Tommy smiles, slightly, at Brett. When he turns back to me he's not smiling anymore. Something twitches in my stomach. He seems to look right through me, as if I'm not really here.

I throw again. Another whiff. I might not be as fast as Randy, but I'm more consistent. And I'm going to start our next game.

Tommy steps out of the box and smacks the end of his bat into the dirt. "I've got sand in my eye!"

Brett stands and takes off his mask and looks at Tommy. "I don't see anything." He shrugs and puts his mask back on.

"I can't see the ball!" Tommy says. "How can I hit if I can't see?"

Brett crouches behind the plate. "Oh, come on. Let's go."

Tommy rubs his eye. Mr. Weeks comes out to take a look. Tommy probably doesn't have anything in his eye. He's buying time. It's a tactical ploy, as David would say.

But then I think of what David said about my fight with Billy. I bet Tommy is embarrassed.

Randy and the boys watch at the fence. What if I strike Tommy out and he gets mad and never looks at me? Besides, this is practice. I don't have to keep throwing strikes.

Tommy steps back into the box. I wind up and throw a slow ball, right down the middle. He smacks the ball into center field.

"God, you threw such a cream puff," Brett yells at me.

Tommy grins at me. I smile back, kind of.

After practice I ride home along Lake Shore Drive. The lake air cools my hot cheeks. This is one of the great things about Lake Michigan. No matter how hot it is, all you have to do is come down to the lake. It's always ten degrees cooler.

Brett has followed me and now rides next to me even though he said his house is the other way. We ride a lot more slowly now. "Is there anything you want?" he says. "That you can't stop thinking about?"

I want lots of things: a new baby-blue Schwinn ten-speed bike. A record player. To erase the day I punched Billy Evans and to send Casey Cunningham back to the other side of town. And I want Sara to call and apologize. "Like a wish?"

"Yeah. A wish that you really want to come true."

I know what I really want. I want Tommy to like me. "I don't know. What do you want?"

"To win the championship! I know we can do it. We've got an awesome team. With you and Randy pitching, me catching, Tommy at second."

My cheeks burn at Tommy's name. Does Brett notice? I change the subject. "What will Randy say when he hears I'm pitching?"

"Who cares? Now we've got two pitchers. We'll probably win the whole thing!"

If Randy thinks he's our best pitcher, then he'll hate that I'm starting. And if he and Tommy are good friends, Tommy won't like it, either.

"What about Tommy?"

Brett glances at me. "What about him?"

Brett can't ever know that I like Tommy or that I'm worried about what Randy will think. "Well, umm, does he pitch?"

"Nah."

We reach my street. "This is where I turn off. My house is down there."

Brett glances down the hill. "Tommy was in my math class last year. He's as dumb as a box of rocks."

Then he takes off down Lake Shore Drive. He calls

back to me, "Put some ice on your shoulder, just in case."

I watch him get smaller and smaller, and I think of a bunch of things I should have said. *Not everyone is as smart as you. Who do you think you are?*

Why can't I ever come up with a decent comeback?

Then I remember how I threw Tommy that cream puff and how he looked so happy, almost relieved, after he belted it.

I pedal fast and faster down the hill. I won't think about this anymore.

6

The next day I sit on the couch with Mimi, who fans herself with *Time* magazine. We're listening to her favorite radio station, jazz out of Chicago.

Mimi and I have an apple pie in the oven. I love that she bakes and plays bridge every Tuesday with her friends from high school and gets her hair done in a beauty salon every week. All normal grandma kinds of things.

"Then," Mimi says, "my grandmother married John May, but she wasn't in love."

I know a lot of her stories. How her great-grandparents came here from England. How she met Gramps in math class when she was fourteen. How after they got married they built their little house all by themselves. In her living room there's a picture of them on their porch, Mimi in a dress with a hammer in her hand.

"Why did she marry him if she didn't love him?"

Mimi reaches into her dress pocket and hands me a mint. In her pockets she keeps secrets, and I'm always surprised by what she pulls out—butterscotches, nail clippers, toothpicks, a fishhook, a recipe cut from the newspaper. Once, a calculator.

"People get married for lots of reasons." She yawns. "Love is only one of them."

She rests her head on the back of the couch and closes her eyes.

I go upstairs and try on my baseball uniform. My left breast still shoots through the o like a bull's-eye. I take off the uniform and put on an old leotard I found in the basement. Unlike my new bra, the leotard flattens my breasts. When I put on my uniform it looks much better.

People get married for lots of reasons.

Usually, I guess, you fall in love and get married. But my mom loved my dad, yet couldn't live with him. Which never made sense. If you love someone, shouldn't you be together, no matter what?

All my friends' parents are married. And Sara's parents are in love. I can tell. Sometimes Dr. Cavanaugh grabs Mrs. Cavanaugh from behind and kisses her neck. And Mrs. Cavanaugh giggles and turns and throws her arms around him.

I haven't gone this long without talking to Sara since last summer when she went on vacation. On their way home she called from a truck stop in St. Joe, and I met her in her driveway when they arrived. Then we got on our bikes and took off before her mom even got out of the car.

Would Sara hang up if I called? Not if I told her about Huey. I go into Mom's room and dial Sara's number. I imagine her hesitating, then sitting on the kitchen counter and eating up every detail I tell her. The phone rings once, twice.

But I hang up before anyone answers. Sara can't keep a secret anymore. And I don't want her to be nice to me only because she wants to meet Huey.

I walk back to my room, take off my uniform and go downstairs. Mimi is still sleeping. I sneak out the front door and stare across Mrs. Minor's yard at Crystal's house. But no way will I risk walking across Mrs. Minor's yard.

She knows things. As a joke one day I dumped a bucket of sand on her driveway while she was at work. When she came home I hid in the hedges and giggled as I watched her sweep it up. It took forever. Then she marched to the hedge.

"I'm not a young woman anymore, Madison Mitchell." She shook her broom at the hedge. "Look at how long it's taken me to clean this up!"

She was right. It *had* taken her a long time. And how had she known it was me? I started to feel really guilty but I was too scared to apologize. I've been avoiding her ever since.

I walk up to Mrs. Minor's lawn, dangle my leg above the grass and let the stiff green blades tickle my foot. Then I walk down the sidewalk and up to Crystal's door and ring the bell.

"Hi, it's me, Madison, the neighbor," I say when Huey answers the door.

I hand him a pair of blue Center City High gym shorts and a green-and-white-striped T-shirt. He holds his cigarette between his lips as he unfolds the clothes. His eyebrows curve up as he stares at the gym shorts.

"Where's Center City?"

"*This* is Center City. Well, it's Long Beach; we're a village in Center City."

Doesn't he even know where he is? If he and Crystal don't talk about things like this, what *do* they talk about?

"Oh, yeah, thanks."

"You're welcome." I look over his shoulder. Newspapers, shoes, socks and beer cans litter the coffee table. A game show is on the TV.

"Where did your band go? Why didn't you finish your tour?"

"My guitarist broke his arm. And Sammy Faig, my drummer, his ma died. They went home. We only had four more shows before the tour ended. Wasn't much of a tour, anyway. Not like it used to be."

"Aren't the people who had tickets to those shows going to be mad? You're going to make it up, right? Like later in the summer?"

Huey blows a smoke ring over my head. "I haven't thought much beyond today."

"Have you and your band ever played in Germany?"

"Yeah, a couple of times. Why?"

"I was born there but we left when I was five. I don't remember it. Except driving to the airport when we were leaving. It was raining and I was happy because I'd never been on a plane and April Clarkson told me you get breakfast, lunch and dinner and little hot face towels that you could take home as souvenirs."

I stop and suck in a breath. I don't tell him about my only other memory of Germany. How I saw my dad outside the screen door and then I blinked and he was in his car driving away, his taillights fading in the dark.

"You sure talk a lot."

My cheeks burn. I *am* talking a lot. I usually don't know what to say.

We turn to the street as Mrs. Minor's car crawls down the hill, up her driveway and into her garage. She begins sweeping her driveway. Is she throwing us dirty looks?

"That woman hates my guts," Huey whispers. I feel a tickle in my stomach as I stare at the hairs on his chest. Now we have something in common. *And* he's taking me into his confidence!

"She hates me, too. Just keep off her grass. She doesn't care about anything else."

Huey raises his eyebrows at me and then steps onto the stoop and looks at Mrs. Minor. "Say, hello there! Nice day we're having, wouldn't you say?"

"How would you know?" Mrs. Minor yells back. "You've been inside all day."

Huey frowns and turns back to me. "Okay, neighbor. I want you to come up with something I can do to get on her good side. Then come back and tell me."

With that he goes inside and shuts the screen door.

*   *   *

That night the team meets under the maple tree next to the field. When I arrive, I see Mr. Weeks talking to Randy. Then Mr. Weeks begins assigning positions. Randy scowls, his arms crossed.

"Madison is our starting pitcher tonight," Mr. Weeks begins. "Randy will play third. For the time being, these two will switch positions every other game."

"What?" A boy says. Others gasp. Randy glares at me.

"Most important," Mr. Weeks says, "just have fun out there."

I start onto the field by myself. Tommy, Randy and the other infielders walk in front of me. Someone says, "*She's* pitching?"

I search the bleachers, where David, Mimi and a few others sit. Small groups of parents are in lawn chairs behind both benches. *Where* is my mom?

"Pitcher is the most important position on the team." Randy turns to me.

I stand on the mound. "*One* of the most important."

"But you've never even played league ball before."

"I know how to pitch."

"I can't believe this. You better not make any mistakes or errors when you're fielding."

Because I'm a girl? "Well, you better not make any, either."

He stomps past me to third base.

I kick the rubber with my toe. He wouldn't be this mad if I were a boy. I sigh and face the plate.

The batter's helmet is too big; he keeps pushing it back on his head. He sticks his tongue out the side of his mouth as he brings back his bat.

54

I pull at the leotard. It digs into the skin under my arms, but it's worth it. HINTON's falls flat across my chest. I re-adjust my cap. My heart is beating wildly. I wipe my cold and clammy hands on my thighs.

"Let's go, Wisconsin," Brett says, squatting. "Bring on the heat!"

I take a deep breath and throw. Too high. Then I throw two more pitches, both balls. I walk him on the fourth pitch. My arms are tight and achy. After a boy singles to left field, I take off David's glove and rub my sweaty hand on my thigh. Why can't I control my pitches out here? This didn't happen to me in practice.

"Ha-ha, she can't pitch," says a boy from the other team. He hangs over the fence, laughing when I glance at him. He's short with a blond crew cut. "The girl can't pitch!"

I glare at him. But I walk the next batter to load the bases. Randy and Doug both groan. Why am I so nervous?

Mr. Weeks stands at the fence, nodding. "It's okay, Madison. Just relax."

The next batter pops out to Tommy.

"She's no pitcher," yells the boy with the crew cut. "She's falling apart."

No way! I kick the rubber once, twice, three times, until my toe stings. What a jerk. I'll show him. I'll strike him out when he's up. I'll shut him up. I'll . . .

Mr. Weeks walks out to the mound, his head down. "Are you okay?"

"That kid won't stop yelling at me."

"He's trying to intimidate you, and it's working. You can't lose your temper. Take a deep breath. Ignore him. I know how well you can pitch."

I nod and he walks back to the bench. I take a couple of deep breaths. Mimi smiles and waves. David, his Wisconsin baseball cap pulled over his eyebrows, gives me a thumbs-up. Mom hurries across the street toward the bleachers. Finally my heartbeat slows.

I strike out the next batter. The boy after that pops out to Doug at shortstop.

When we're up, I hit a fly ball that bounces past the left fielder for a triple and knocks in two runs. The boy with the crew cut yells at me a few more times, but I ignore him. Pretty soon I don't hear him at all.

At the plate, I walk in the third inning and single in the fifth. I'm in a groove on the mound, and I pitch the entire game. Even though Tommy makes two errors at second, we win easily, five to nothing.

Afterward, we sit under the tree, hot and sweaty. A couple of the younger boys build a castle out of branches and mud they make from pouring Kool-Aid into the dirt.

"We were pretty awesome out there," Brett says. "How does your arm feel?"

"Great." My underarms are sore from where the leotard rubbed against me, but I grin at him. Once we got going, it was fun, like volleyball. Working as a team, cheering each other. Maybe at the next game I won't be so nervous. I'd better not be.

Randy and Tommy sit off to the side with Doug and Brian and a few others. Every so often one of them turns and looks at me. What are they saying? But I don't care, now that the game's over. I won't let anyone bother me.

Everyone played well. Tommy and Brett both had hits.

Doug hit a home run in the sixth. Randy was good at third. He picks up his glove and walks toward me.

"Just so you know, I'm pitching in the next game."

Everyone knows we're going to alternate pitching. But he walks away before I can think of anything to say. "What's his problem?" I ask Brett.

"He wanted to be the star this year, I guess." He slurps the Kool-Aid from his cup.

"What does everyone else think about me pitching?"

Brett shrugs. "We all just want to win."

I watch Tommy get up and follow Randy to the bike rack. The last light of the day pokes through the branches and shines on his back. Even from here, he seems to glow. When I look at Brett, he's frowning at me.

"Come on, Mad, let's go," David yells. "I got to meet D.J. and Artie."

"See you." I run to Mom and David, my sweaty hand still inside his glove.

"Take a look at the newspaper," Mimi says to me late the next afternoon.

I glance at the front-page headline, *No Change in Status of Hostages*, and open to the sports page. There, at the bottom, is a two-column headline: *Long Beach Girl Stars in Town League Debut.*

> The battle of the sexes has come to Long Beach! Twelve-year-old Madison Mitchell became the first girl in southern Michigan to play league baseball when she debuted for Hinton's Grocery on Tuesday.

And what a debut it was. Allowing just two hits, Mitchell pitched a near-flawless game. She had a single and also knocked in two runs with a triple as Hinton's ran past Karwick Pharmacy, 5–0.

But the debut came with controversy. Said one parent, "She'll psych out the other team. Everyone will worry about hurting her and getting blamed because she's a girl. She'll have an unfair advantage and we should think about whether this is a good idea or not."

But according to John Weeks, Hinton's coach, this doesn't seem to be a problem.

"Madison is tough. She's one of the best natural baseball players I've ever seen, girl or boy. Everyone is just going to have to get used to this."

Battle of the sexes! I'm not some crazy feminist. I'm playing because I was bored and David pushed me and because, well, because I don't really know why. Because it's something I do well, and that feels pretty great. But what will everyone think now? What will my *friends* think?

I slump into a chair and pull my shirt away from my raw underarms. I glance up at Mimi. "Why is this such a big deal? I'm not a women's libber or anything."

Mimi turns off the water at the sink and rubs her hand on a towel. "So you're bothered not by the fact that you're in the paper, but by the feminist slant."

I cringe when she says *feminist*. My mom uses this word all the time. It sounds like something that should be on the side of a Kotex box.

"Well, yeah," I say. "Wouldn't you hate that?"

Mimi stares at me, her hand on her hip. She takes a long

time to answer. But she's not like my mom. She doesn't run fund-raisers for Planned Parenthood or march in protests. She never makes a big deal, as Mom always does, about things like being the only woman on law review.

"If I were playing baseball just to play baseball, then I guess I'd be upset by those references, too," Mimi says finally.

There. At least Mimi understands.

"This is so new, girls playing ball, people don't know what to make of it," she says. "All sorts of opportunities are opening up for girls. But it takes time. It wasn't too long ago that girls couldn't wear pants to school. They had to wear dresses and skirts."

"Well, thank God I wasn't alive then!"

The next day the newspaper runs two letters to the editor about me.

> Madison Mitchell sounds like a darn good baseball player. But if we continue to let her play league ball, then every girl will want to play, and that's just not fair to the boys. Girls will bring down the level of play. Boys should be allowed to play by themselves.
>
> Tom Beldon

> Madison Mitchell is a wonderful athlete, and we should all celebrate her talents and spunk. It's a real treat to watch her play. And what a great role model for girls everywhere!
>
> Jan Post, Lakeshore Junior High School

It's nice that Mrs. Post called me wonderful, but I keep rereading the other letter. *Girls will bring down the level of play.* I certainly didn't bring down any levels. I didn't make one mistake, one error. I can play with the boys just fine.

Still, when the paper has two more letters the next night and three the night after that—three supporting me, two against—I worry. What if I don't play as well as I did? This will be my first time playing third base. What if I make an error? But no one accused Tommy of bringing down any levels when he made errors.

On the night of our next game, we gather by the maple tree. I listen to Mr. Weeks as I count the people. So far there are thirty-seven in the bleachers. More stand along the sidelines. Sara and I never saw this many people when we rode our bikes past this field last summer.

David and Mimi sit in the bleachers. Mrs. Post chases her two-year-old along the first-base line. My eyes dart through the crowd. How can Mom be late again? I can't begin until she's here. Which is crazy. She doesn't know anything about baseball.

"Okay, let's take the field," Mr. Weeks says.

"There are so many people," Donny says.

The bleachers are still filling. People start lining up behind the benches. Someone in the crowd yells, "Where's the girl?" Prickles race up my arms.

Mr. Weeks squeezes my shoulder and looks at everyone. "I know what all of you can do. Just go out, play ball and have fun, okay?"

I pull at the leotard. My underarms had just begun to

heal and now the leotard digs back into my skin. We run out to the field. Randy takes the mound. I stop on third and turn.

I pull back my shoulders. I pound my fist into the pocket of David's glove. I can do this. It's just third base. But the infield is full of tiny potholes and rocks.

I've fielded lots of balls while pitching or playing first base with David and his friends. I know you have to move to the ball so your glove is on the ground, between your legs. That way if you misjudge the ball or it takes a bad bounce your body will be behind the glove to stop it.

I look at Brian at first base. I can make the long throw. Most batters are right-handed. More balls will come to me here than at first base or pitching. A lot more.

Last night David brought me here and hit balls to me. A couple of times the balls took bad bounces and hit me in the shoulder, the thigh. Which stung like crazy. But at least I didn't get a bloody nose or get hit in the chest. I'd die if that happened in a game.

Tommy bends forward, his elbows on his thighs. Brett squats behind the plate. Randy's first pitch is high for a ball. The batter hits the next pitch and a slow grounder comes up the third-base line. I get into position, catch the ball in my glove and throw it to first base. Out. But I wince at how sharp the pain is when the leotard cuts into my skin.

The crowd explodes in cheers. "Attagirl!" someone yells. Tommy nods at me. Doug raises his eyebrows. I pound my fist into my glove.

Randy walks the next two batters and strikes out the

two after that. When we're up, Brett walks and Doug pops out. Tommy singles and then I'm up. As I walk to the plate I see my mom hurrying through the parking lot. *Finally.*

I swing big and miss the first pitch. Someone yells, "What a whiff!" I step out of the box. What would my dad tell me? But then I remember what David said when he first started pitching to me. *Don't always go for the fences. Just get on base.*

I let the next pitch go and swing at the third and hit a grounder up the middle that goes between the center fielder's legs for a double. The crowd cheers. Brett pumps his fist as he crosses home plate. I score when Randy hits a double. Before the other team gets three outs, we're up three to nothing.

In the third inning I hit a shallow fly just over the second baseman's head that sends home Brett and Tommy. At third, I catch a line drive and field another grounder. The leotard bites into my skin, but I make the throw to first.

By the last inning, we lead eight to one, even though Randy has walked a dozen batters. He throws, and *crack*, the ball comes at me. But I don't react quickly enough and have to reach into the dirt on the far side of my left foot to make a scooping catch. I barely get the throw to first on time. I suck in a breath as the leotard cuts me.

We win, and the crowd cheers. "Way to go, Madison!" someone yells.

We huddle on the mound, congratulating each other. After Brian says "great game" to me, Randy sneers at him until he slinks away. Donny and Doug are avoiding me, too. Has Randy turned them against me?

This makes me so angry that I turn to charge after him and practically run into Tommy. I stop. I've never been this close to him. He has to look at me now, but I want to make sure. "Nice game," I say.

He smiles. His eyes are so blue and his skin looks warm. I feel something tingle through my stomach and knees. "You too," he says. He walks off to the sidelines.

"You like him," Brett says. "I can tell. Too bad. He's got a girlfriend."

I roll my eyes. But I feel as if someone has rearranged the field underneath me and I can't get my balance. Of course. Tommy is sure to have a girlfriend. I run over to Mom and David.

"What were you doing with that last play?" David asks. "You should have gotten behind the ball."

"It just came at me so fast."

"Very nice hitting, Madison." Mom puts her arm around my shoulder.

I bury my face in her shirt, close my eyes and breathe in. The time flew by! Why was I so nervous? And who is Tommy's girlfriend?

When I open my eyes, I see Sara and Gina behind the backstop and I pull away from Mom. Did they come to see me? Maybe things aren't so bad. But I don't move.

Sara and Gina wear matching blue tube tops and cut-offs. They're talking with two older boys who straddle dirt bikes. Gina lightly punches one in the arm. They laugh.

Casey walks to them from the other side of the bleachers. Sara and Gina step back to make way for her. Casey stands in the middle.

Then I feel as if everyone has stopped talking and moving and breathing. And this aching pulls at me. I think of how Sara and I put our feet on top of each other's rafts to keep from separating as we floated in the lake. How we sat at the counter in our kitchen, talking with my mom. How sometimes, each in our own house, we'd watch the same TV show while talking on the phone.

We've been together every summer since we were eight and old enough to ride all over Long Beach by ourselves. Does she miss me, too?

I stuff my cap into my glove and run my fingers through my curls. Why are they laughing? I should walk over, say hi. I bet my shoulders would look too big in a tube top.

But maybe they came to watch the boys, not me. I hide on the other side of Mom. The leotard digs into my raw skin. Two boys ride by on bikes, one pointing. *Look at that girl in a boy's uniform!* Is that what he's saying?

"Here, I got you some lemonade," Brett says.

"Thanks." I drink it slowly and close my eyes. I look up again. No one is staring at me, and the girls have gone.

Tommy walks off toward the parking lot. When I look at Brett he's frowning. But I don't care. Tommy smiled at me.

Later I sit on the roof, holding out my shirt so the air can cool the raw spots under my arms. The neighborhood is quiet and still. In the fading light I see Rex, sleeping on our driveway. Beach balls, buckets and shovels have been left all over the Tullivers' yard.

Mrs. Minor pulls a bucket of lawn tools onto her driveway. She examines a red rosebush that climbs the side of her garage; then she snips off one little leaf.

She turns to Crystal's house, her hands on her hips.

Maybe she's scowling at that awful, weed-infested, knee-high-grass yard. I sit up. I know how Huey can get on Mrs. Minor's good side.

7

The next day I sit on the front steps. Mimi has gone in for a nap and the air is so hot that I sweat without moving.

D.J. and Artie, David's best friends, sit with me, waiting for David. They're too busy with summer jobs to hang out every day. We haven't played baseball in the Phillipses' field since last summer.

"This lady put the car into reverse instead of neutral and backed up into the console and shut the car wash down." D.J. throws his arms in the air. "Day off for us."

"But it's a day without pay, you meathead." Artie takes a water balloon from the stash they've just filled and throws it at a tree. It misses and explodes on the driveway.

"Stop wasting them," D.J. says. Artie grins.

I laugh. I put my elbows on my knees and lean forward

so my shirt falls away from the raw spots. If I stay like this maybe it will stop hurting.

"What's taking him so long?" D.J. glances back at the house.

"You know it takes a long time for Mr. Serious to look good," Artie says.

I laugh again. They're meeting our neighbor Tina Phillips and her friends at the beach. Tina is a cheerleader with long, straight blond hair and big breasts. All three have had crushes on her since junior high, although none of them would admit it, especially David.

"What's going on, Madwoman?" D.J. asks. Madwoman, Madness, Mad Hatter. In the course of an hour it's possible to hear all of these nicknames. I smile. D.J. says, "Heard you were the star pitcher the other night."

"Yeah," Artie says. "And star hitter."

I straighten. "Who told you that?"

"I don't know," Artie says. "Everyone's talking about you."

"Those boys must have been peeing in their pants!" D.J. laughs and slaps me on the back. I frown. *Who* is talking about this?

David walks out the door, a towel in his hands. His hair is combed. "Ready?"

"Whoa, check that out," Artie says.

Crystal walks down the driveway toward her car. She's dressed in cutoffs, a tight red tube top, and high-heeled sandals. She walks slowly, her arms swinging at her sides.

"What happened to *her*?" D.J. whistles softly.

"She still lives there alone?" Artie asks.

I glance at David. I don't want him to know I've been talking to Huey. But mostly I don't want Artie and D.J. to know about Huey. Then it will be all over Long Beach.

"Yep, all alone," I say.

"Well, she's hot," Artie says.

"You can say that again," D.J. says.

"Well, she's hot," Artie says. D.J. punches him in the shoulder. Then they take turns punching each other.

What makes Crystal hot? Her clothes? Those high heels? The way she walks? She gets in the car and drives away.

Artie and D.J. stand. Artie says, "When's your next game? We'll come."

I glance at D.J.'s stomach, so flat under his tank top. Unlike David, he got tall this year. And he has muscles. My cheeks redden and I look away.

"Mad's the star," Artie says. "She struck out fifteen boys the other night."

"Well, actually it was nine," David says.

"Nine?" Artie throws up his arms. "Awesome, Madness!"

"Remember the first time she homered over the shed?" D.J. asks. "What were you, like eight or something?"

"She was ten, same age as the rest of us when we did it." David walks down the steps and around the side of the house.

"We're out of here, Madness." D.J. stands, lifts the bucket full of water balloons and starts down the steps. Artie reaches over and pulls one out. Then he runs into the yard, turns and throws. It explodes on D.J.'s back.

"Artie, I'm gonna get you for that!" D.J. chases him

around the back of the house, the bucket swinging at his side.

They left some empty balloons on the porch. I stuff a handful into my pocket, walk to the end of the driveway and look up the hill. A girl rides her bike on Lake Shore Drive, slowly, glancing down the hill toward me. Sara!

I run down the driveway, climb on my bike and ride up the hill. I turn onto Lake Shore Drive. The girl is up ahead, but as I get closer I see that her bike is blue, not green. It's not Sara. I stop pedaling and my bike slows, then stops. I stand on the hot pavement, the sun sharp against my back.

Before I know what I'm doing, I'm riding toward town.

In Hinton's I stare at Crystal over the top of a magazine. She looks different. Her reddish brown hair is pulled behind her ears instead of hanging in her face. She wears lipstick, black eyeliner and a silver necklace with a big sparkly heart on the end. She's smiling, but the smile isn't on her lips. It's in her eyes.

I grab a candy bar and get into her line. My mom always waits in Crystal's line, even if it's the longest in the store. She always asks Crystal a bunch of questions. Have you heard from your dad? When are you starting night school? Crystal barely answers and I don't know why my mom even bothers.

"Hi," I say when it's my turn.

Crystal picks up the chocolate bar and punches some numbers into the cash register. Her breasts push out over the tube top, and she doesn't seem at all concerned about hiding them. Does Huey think she's hot?

"That's twenty-five cents." Crystal stares over my shoulder.

I watch her lips as she says this. They're thick and puffy and colored a deep dark red. I imagine them pressed to Huey's lips.

Crystal didn't play sports or hang out with us. She's older; I never paid much attention to her. Then one day about six months after her mom died, I overheard Mom tell Mimi that Crystal's dad was moving to Ohio. "Leaving Crystal behind," she said.

Leaving her behind! Why? Because she was a maniac?

That afternoon I sat in the pine tree behind her house for an hour, watching, waiting for a chance to see if she was okay. Finally I walked around the side of the house and saw her through her bedroom window. She was reading a magazine filled with naked people. She smoked a cigarette as she read, then flicked it out the window when she was finished.

It landed at my feet, and I stared at the thick red imprint from her lips circling the end of the cigarette. When I glanced back up, Crystal was staring at me. "What are you spying on? Get out of here, you little tomboy!"

I stomped off and vowed I'd never worry about her again.

Now I hand her a quarter. "So what's new? How have you been?"

Crystal looks at me for the first time. She blows a bubble with her gum and it pops all over her thick lips. With her tongue she gathers the gum in one big swipe.

"How is everything here at Hinton's?" I don't know how to bring up Huey's name, but I want to do it nonchalantly, as if it's completely natural.

"What do you want?" Crystal asks.

"What's Huey Milligan doing in your house?"

Crystal's eyes shoot wide open. She tightens her top earring, a skull, and glances toward the courtesy counter before leaning over the register to me.

"Listen, you little snoop. You better not be blabbing this all over Long Beach. Huey don't want any trouble or people hanging around."

"I won't tell anyone. I could've told lots of people but I haven't."

Crystal straightens and begins chewing again. She glances at the woman unloading groceries behind me, then leans across the register again, frowning. "I mean it. Do you *understand*?"

I grab my candy bar and run off. I'm not a little kid. I can keep a secret.

I ride as fast as I can, the wind streaming through my curls. It's much later than I realized. I park in front of the garage and peek in the window but Mimi isn't on the couch. She's in the backyard, shelling peas into a metal bowl. I lower myself next to her.

Surely she can hear my heart pounding from the ride. I throw back my shoulders and sit up. I can lie. I can say there was an emergency.

I have to think, so I reach for a pod. The peas make a loud *ping* when I dump them into the bowl. Still Mimi doesn't say anything. I think about the times she stayed with me when I was sick and Mom was working. How she's always such a good listener.

"I'm sorry, Mimi." I can lie to Mom, but not to Mimi.

"Baseball practice is the only place you're supposed to go until your mom gives the okay. Remember?"

I feel my cheeks burn. We sit quietly. "Are you going to tell Mom?"

She sighs. "No, as long as you promise not to take off like that again."

I nod.

"The newspaper is on the table," Mimi says, nudging my shoulder.

In the kitchen I glance at the front-page headline, *Hostage Situation Unchanged*, and open to the sports. The article about our game is only three paragraphs long. My name is there, for a double and a single, but I'm glad Brett and Tommy are mentioned for good games. Randy, too. I turn to the letters.

There are three. Mrs. Tulliver writes that with no "summer sports options," why shouldn't I be allowed to play? Someone else calls me a trailblazer. In the last letter, a woman writes that it's time our town talked about a girls' softball league.

I push away from the table.

It's just baseball.

8

Mom knows something is wrong. Otherwise she'd be working in the family room, the way she always does after dinner. She wouldn't stand in bare feet at the edge of the driveway, asking a million questions.

"Are you feeling okay?"

I wind up and throw a tennis ball into the square on the garage door. I don't wear the leotard or my bra, so my underarm doesn't hurt. I glance at Mom. If I keep ignoring her, maybe she'll go back into the house.

"I found this. I thought you'd need it." She holds out the booklet that came with my mood ring. "Under the couch."

"Thank you." I take it with my free hand. She glances at my glove, and I'm glad it covers the hand where I usually wear my ring.

"Do you miss your friends?"

I shrug.

"Are you worried about all these letters to the editor?"

With her curly hair and gauze shirts, she looks like a hippie, especially barefoot. She's always barefoot.

"I don't know."

"Are you worried that everyone's going to label you a feminist?"

"A what?"

"You heard me."

I stop and look at her. "I'm playing because I want to. I'm not some *feminist*."

"Okay." Mom bites her lip and glances at the house. "Okay, well, I have to go back inside. I have to be in court tomorrow."

She hesitates, and I keep throwing. Then she walks into the house.

The minute she's gone, I wish her back. I don't want to upset her. I don't know why I can't talk to her now or why words like *feminist* bother me so much. But I can just imagine how Billy or Casey would laugh if they heard my mom. *Feminist?* No other moms in Long Beach talk like that or dress the way she does.

I throw a little bit longer, then go up to my room and open the window. Huey is sitting on Crystal's back stoop. Then she opens the door and sits next to him.

I slide out the window and scoot across the roof to the TV antenna tower. Then I climb down the tower ladder, which is attached to the house, run across the dune and crawl under the pine tree.

I'm still too far away to hear them talking. But Crystal isn't happy, not the way she stares at the ground and shrugs whenever Huey says something.

Then Huey stands and pulls Crystal up. He says, loudly, "Oh, baby, baby, *baby*," and wraps his arms around her. Her neck bends and Huey's body closes over her and then they kiss this most incredible kiss.

That's it. They're in love. I should give them privacy. But I can't stop watching. Those big, fleshy lips of Crystal's, and Huey's arms swallowing her. After Sara kissed Nick Surowiec behind the Dairy Queen last year, she said their front teeth kept colliding. But Crystal kisses Huey as if it's the most natural thing she's ever done. As if she's been doing it for years.

Would it feel like that to kiss Tommy?

I walk back across the dune and climb up the TV tower. Mom calls my name as I scoot across the roof. I hurl myself through the window and replace the screen just as she knocks.

She opens the door and glances at the window. I bring my hand to my cheek.

"Have you had to answer a lot of questions about your bruise?" She tries to touch me, but I back up and frown.

"No."

"Well, your punishment is almost over and you'll be free to see the girls."

I shrug and flop on my bed and open the mood ring booklet. *Black. You are feeling excess stress and anxiety.* No kidding.

9

"Don't forget to push off with your right foot. Let that give you power." David puts his mask back on and crouches in front of the garage.

As I throw I think about last night, how Crystal and Huey's bodies fit together when they kissed. The ball sails toward David's head. He ducks, and it crashes into the garage and rolls down the driveway.

"Maddie. You're not paying attention."

I pick up the ball, then stare into David's mitt and push off with my foot as I let go. The ball explodes into his mitt.

"That's it." David winces and tosses it back.

"How about a curveball?" I try to flick my wrist when I throw, the way Randy did the other night.

David catches the ball and stands. "You're way too

76

young. You gotta wait until you're older. Otherwise you'll ruin your arm."

"Randy throws a curve, and he's the same age as me."

"Yeah, and he's going to regret it someday."

We both turn when Mom comes out the back door. She carries her briefcase and her sandals. Already the temperature is in the eighties.

"The bottoms of your feet are going to get dirty," I say. How can she go to work like that?

"Oh, no one will notice or care." She laughs. Then she starts going through her briefcase, mumbling, "Now, what did I do with that notebook?"

"Good luck today," David says, pushing up his mask. Mom smiles, then glances at me.

"Yeah, good luck," I say. Although I doubt she'll need it.

"Thanks. What are you going to do today, honey?" she asks me.

"Go to practice. I can't do anything else, remember? I'm *grounded*."

She pulls a notebook from her briefcase. "Your punishment will soon be over. I'll see you later this afternoon."

She drives up the hill and disappears and I feel an ache in my chest, but I don't know why.

"Come on, Mad." David puts on the mask, crouches and holds out the glove.

"Tell me what Dad was like."

"I don't have anything new since the last time you asked," he says.

I cross my arms. "Do you think he's in Iran right now?"

"Oh, God, I don't know."

I think about the stats David got from Wisconsin's athletic department. Dad didn't make one error in four years while playing third base. I bet he never got nervous. I bet he always knew what to do. "Why do you think he was such a good baseball player?"

"Why are you asking all these questions? Come on. A few more pitches, then I've got to get to work. I don't want to be late."

I stand there, hands on my hips.

"Okay," David says. "I'll tell you something. He had really big hands. He wasn't that tall. Like me, I guess. But his hands were huge. When I was eight I saw him palm a basketball. He just picked it up and held it in one hand."

I picture Dad standing in his army fatigues and palming a basketball. It's not much of an image. What did he do with it? Did he pick it up with his right or left hand? Maybe he was teaching David how to put backspin on a jump shot.

I smile. It's something new, something I hadn't imagined Dad doing before, and I'm glad of that.

At practice, the bleachers are empty and no one stands along the sidelines. On the mound, the sun beats down and the dust kicks up every time I push off. This is how it should be. Just the team, the balls, the bats. I wind up, then turn my foot along the side of the rubber and throw.

"Bull's-eye!" Brett says as he sends the ball back. I glance toward left field, where Randy is pitching to Mr.

Weeks. Tommy is out in right, hitting fly balls to the out-fielders. They're too far away to hear us.

I kick at the dirt behind the rubber. I'm wearing my bra, not the leotard. What a difference. No rubbing. No pain. But my uniform top is way tighter than this new baggy T-shirt. I don't know how I'll pitch wearing the leotard again.

I throw again. Donny swings and misses.

"Strike!" Doug says from shortstop. He nods at me when I glance at him.

Before practice, Brett said Randy told everyone it should be against the rules for girls to play in the league. He's trying to get them mad at me. But now that we're playing and Randy isn't here, it sure doesn't seem as if anyone is mad at me.

My body is loose. My arm is strong. I turn when I hear Doug and Brian arguing.

"I can slide farther than you," Doug says.

"Yeah, *right*," Brian says from first base. "I'm a better slider."

Donny rests his bat on his shoulder and says, "Come on, guys."

I walk over to second base. "Let's see who's the best slider."

"That's not what we're supposed to do," Brian says.

"It's okay," I say. Brett pulls off his catching gear as he hurries toward us.

Everyone lines up behind second base. I stand halfway between second and third. "Okay, I'll make a mark at the point where you start your slide."

Brett runs toward third, leans back and slides, feetfirst. I drag my heel in the dirt, marking a spot about eight feet out. Then it's Brian's turn, Donny's and Doug's. When it's my turn, I hesitate. I've never slid before. Maybe I'll surprise them and go headfirst, like I've seen the pros do on TV.

"Madison, go!" Brian says. "What if Mr. Weeks sees us?"

I take off for third, throw out my hands and dive headfirst. But when I hit the dirt, I die there, stuck. Pain shoots through my breasts. Dirt goes down the front of my shirt, up my nose, into my mouth.

Then the pain passes and I sit up.

The boys laugh, trying to be quiet, then louder. Doug doubles over, howling. I crack up, too.

"Nice belly flop. Way to go, Wisconsin." Brett laughs as he puts on his shin guards.

I wipe my mouth on my sleeve, then spit. My saliva is dark brown. "Yuck!"

"Nice lunch," Brett says. We can't stop laughing.

"Here they come!" Brian shouts. We hurry back to our positions. I throw a pitch as hard as I can. Donny swings and misses. Then he cracks up again.

Behind Brett a man sits in the middle of the empty bleachers. He's dressed in a short-sleeved shirt and tie. He waves, but I don't know who he is.

"What's going on here?" Mr. Weeks says. He and Randy stop next to me.

"We were just—" Brian begins.

"I was having lunch," I say, loudly enough for everyone to hear. They all snicker. Randy glances around.

Mr. Weeks chuckles. "Okay, well, let's get back to business."

I smile at Brett, then the others. Tommy grabs a bat. I glance down; I'm covered with dirt. For once I'm glad Tommy isn't looking at me.

After practice I head out on my bike and the man from the bleachers stops me. "Hi. I'm Mike Carter. I've been admiring your pitching. And sliding." He chuckles.

I shake his hand. He's tall and nearly bald and wears black-framed glasses that make his eyes look too big for his face.

"I'm the sports editor at the *News-Dispatch*. Well, actually I'm the editor, the writer and the copy editor, too. Pretty small operation. How did you get to be such a good baseball player?"

"My brother taught me," I say. Reporters make judgments, Huey said. But Mr. Carter doesn't look as if he'd do anything mean. I squeeze my handlebars.

"Oh, yes, David. Manages the high school team. Keen sense of the game. Thought he'd end up playing. Even with that unorthodox throwing style."

"Kind of sidearm."

"Yeah, yeah, that's it. He knows the game inside and out."

I smile. David *does* know everything about baseball. I let go of the handlebars.

"You seem to know everything about it, too. Got everyone in town in an uproar over this." He chuckles again. I put my hands back on the handlebars.

I should tell him this isn't a battle. I shift my feet and

wonder what my mom is doing right now. Brett and the others watch me. "It's just baseball."

"Sure it's just baseball, and you're really good. I want to write an article about you, first girl and all. I'll be in touch. We can sit down and talk."

I don't want to be in an article. But I just stand there, staring at him.

"Nice to meet you." He walks away. The boys hurry over to me.

"Why'd he want to talk to you?" Doug asks.

"He's going to write about you, isn't he?" Brett folds his arms.

What will he ask? At least I don't have a brother who is in jail and people who are suing me. Will he ask about Dad? I twist the handlebars until my knuckles turn white.

Tommy stands next to me. When he smiles, I feel my heart beating in my chest, my ears, even my ankles. "Wow, Madison. You're so lucky. I wish someone would write an article about me. You're going to be famous!"

Randy stomps off to the parking lot.

Maybe it won't be so bad after all.

Later I stand in front of Mom's mirror in my Speedo bathing suit. Both knees are scabbed over from a bike wreck a couple of weeks ago. My curls are wild in the humidity. But at least my breasts, which are so much bigger than my friends' breasts, have stopped growing for the time being.

I sit on Mom's bed. Her room is full of driftwood sculptures and painted rocks I made. Colored bottles washed up with the waves. Magazines and books stacked in piles. Mimi calls her a packrat. Our garage is like this, too, filled with things Mom rescued from the beach—an old grill, lawn chairs, a giant inner tube.

I stand and slip on one of her nicer skirts, a blue one with tiny white flowers. I scoop my curls on top of my head and pose—one leg out with a pointed toe, my free hand across my chest. I tilt my head, the way I saw Crystal do, and part my lips. I try to picture Tommy standing next to me, his teeth shining, his hand behind my back.

But it doesn't work. Maybe if I put on earrings. Lipstick. Because when I look at myself, I don't quite see a girl. At least not the kind Crystal is. Or Casey. Or even Mom.

Billy Evans is right, I'm a tomboy. Can't I be a tomboy and wear makeup?

I run my finger across the skirt. It's soft and silky but there's a tear along the hem. She should buy some new clothes, like what Sara's mom wears—pantsuits or white tennis skirts with razor-sharp pleats. Maybe she could stay home and play tennis like the other moms.

I take off the skirt and toss it on the bed where I found it. I peek down the stairs. Mimi is asleep on the couch, listening to afternoon jazz. I tiptoe out the door, walk to Crystal's and ring the bell.

Huey opens the door, frowning. "What do you want?"

"What's the matter?"

"What's the idea, bothering Crystal while she was at work?" Huey shakes his hair out of his eyes. "You got her all upset."

"I . . . I . . . I wasn't bothering her."

83

"She said you were bothering her."

I lick my lips. "I didn't mean anything."

Huey scrunches his forehead. He looks as if he just woke up. "Look, Crystal doesn't need any problems." His voice is softer.

"Don't you think I know that, what with her mom dead and her dad in Ohio?" I blurt.

Huey steps onto the stoop, his body drooping forward, his head down.

He's sorry he's been mean to me. I suddenly feel in charge. "I came to tell you that I know how to get on Mrs. Minor's good side. Mow Crystal's lawn."

He sighs and sits on the stoop, holding his head in his hands. "I'm sorry. I'm just . . . Well, I have writer's block and I'm a little on edge right now."

A thrill starts up my back. He's taking me into his confidence again. *Writer's block.* It sounds so Hollywoodish. I imagine him sitting at Crystal's desk, gnawing on a pencil and doodling in the margins of a notebook. That's what I do when I can't think what to write. I sit. "How long have you had writer's block?"

He looks at me and chuckles. "Oh, years."

"Wow. What are you going to do about it?"

"That's the question, my friend. That's the question." Huey sighs again and digs his toe into the sand next to the sidewalk. "How did Crystal's mom die?"

Hasn't Crystal told him? What do they talk about when she comes home? I stare at his lips and think about him kissing Crystal. Are they going to get married? Move to California?

84

"Well, I don't really know. One night Crystal is running around in a snowstorm, and the next thing I know, her mom is in the hospital, and then three days later she dies. This was three years ago. I was only nine."

I hope Huey doesn't ask why Crystal was running around in a snowstorm. I don't want to be the one to tell him that she wore only a nightgown.

"But you don't know how she died?"

That night as my mom headed out into the storm with a blanket, she told David to take me upstairs. I tried to see from my window, but it was dark, the glass frosted over. "No. She was in a coma for three days. Then my mom told me that her heart finally gave out. So I guess something was wrong with her heart."

I've been so focused on how crazy Crystal was, running in circles under the streetlight in only a nightgown—a summer nightgown, no less, sleeveless with frills along the hem—I haven't thought much about how Mrs. Adams died. Did she have a heart attack? Did she have a heart attack right in front of Crystal?

Huey points to my cheek. "It's looking better. That must have been some punch."

I drop my eyes. He never said anything about my bruise, so I assumed he hadn't noticed.

"Or did you get that playing baseball?"

"How do you know about that?" My eyes dart up to his face.

"Read about it. I figure there can't be too many twelve-year-old Madisons around here. That had to be you making the debut." He chuckles.

"This reporter wants to write an article about me, but I don't want to do it."

"Why not?"

"Because I don't want him to call me a trailblazer or role model or anything."

Huey nods. "Well, maybe you *should* talk to him. Set the record straight about who you are, you know? The secret to dealing with the press is being prepared. Think before you talk. Have a lot of dramatic pauses."

"Dramatic pauses?"

"Yeah, tilt your head, scrunch up your eyebrows so it looks like you're in deep thought. Hesitate. Count to ten. Take a breath. And don't say anything stupid."

I never seem to know the right thing to say. But I nod.

Huey bends down and pulls a weed from the sand. "Can't I hire someone to do this yard?"

"No. You have to do it. And Mrs. Minor has to see you do it."

I smile. Maybe he can help me, too.

10

When I get home, Mimi is on the porch, fanning herself with the newspaper. "How's the rock star today?"

I sit next to her. "How do you know about him?"

"David told your mom and me."

I knew he couldn't keep a secret!

"He and Crystal are, you know, a couple. I think they're in love." I look at Mimi because I'm not so sure about this.

Mimi sighs. "Love can be a strange and wonderful thing."

She reaches into her dress pocket and pulls out a butterscotch for me.

"Was your love for Gramps strange and wonderful?"

Mimi smiles. "We had a forever love. He was my best friend. We argued. We loved. And after more than thirty years of marriage we still looked forward to seeing each other every morning."

I glance at Mimi. Gramps has been gone a long time. "You must miss him."

"Every moment of every day." She sighs and puts the candy wrapper in her pocket.

"I guess my parents didn't have a forever love, huh?"

Mimi pauses and tilts her head. "There are different kinds of love. There's physical love and infatuation. There's love based on mutual respect and friendship. Sometimes love is happy and safe. Often times it's painful and disappointing."

Is she talking about my parents?

She crunches down on her butterscotch and stares out into the street. "Your parents loved each other very hard. But I think they just grew too far apart."

Rex walks up the driveway and sits at my feet, panting. I scratch under his collar. Mimi smiles and pets Rex. "Come on. Let's get this poor guy some water."

Two mornings later I'm in the kitchen with David. He stands at the table, the newspaper spread before him.

Mom comes into the kitchen, hair wet from her shower. She stuffs papers into her briefcase. "Are you ready, David?"

He nods. "They've got a write-up about your case in the court report."

"Hmm." She slips her feet into sandals.

"This article makes it sound like the judge was surprised you won."

"I'm a bit surprised, too."

"You're kidding, right?" I ask. They both look at me. "Don't you always win?"

"Heavens, no." She stops moving and looks at me. "What would ever make you think that?"

David laughs. I feel the heat rise to my cheeks. I shrug.

"You believed the woman was innocent. And you were fully prepared." David smiles at me, as if to say *I know everything about this and you don't.*

"True, but that doesn't mean we were sure to win," she says. "You have to consider the case from the other side. You always have to anticipate what the prosecution will present."

Now it's my turn to smile at David.

Usually when she and David talk about work, I tune them out. It always sounds so complicated and hard to understand.

"Will you tell me about the case?" I follow her to the screen door. How'd she win?

"Oh, yes, sure, but I'm so late now." She checks her watch. I hold open the screen door as she rushes out. Halfway down the driveway she turns. "Why don't you ask the girls over after the game? You've been grounded long enough."

I bite my lip. It's been almost three weeks since school ended. Not once has anyone called.

She waits, but I just look at her wet hair, piled on top of her head and secured with a pencil. I'd never go out in public with a pencil stuck in my hair.

"Please don't be late for my game tonight."

She blows me a kiss and I shut the door. I imagine the kiss landing *splat* on the screen.

By five o'clock, when it's time to leave for the game, the temperature is still in the nineties.

I wear my bathing suit under my uniform, nice and snug. After the game I can go straight to the lake.

Tommy and I are the first to arrive. I keep glancing at him as I put my bike in the rack, but he doesn't notice me. My bathing suit feels like a heating pad.

He starts to walk away.

"Aren't you going to lock your bike?" I ask.

"Huh?"

"Don't you think someone could steal it? It's a great bike."

And it is. Schwinn, powder blue, ten-speed. Brand-new. Exactly the kind of bike I've always wanted.

He nods. "It's fast, too."

"Do you want to warm up?"

He shrugs. We begin throwing along the third-base line. My feet feel tingly and light. I like the sound the ball makes every time I catch it. I hear voices and laughter and the smack of more balls against leather. But I don't take my eyes off Tommy and the ball.

"You should be throwing with me." Brett stands next to me.

"Why?"

"He doesn't have a catcher's mitt. He's not going to catch you during the game."

"That's okay."

Tommy throws a goofy sidearm ball and laughs. I catch it and laugh, too.

"This team we're playing is good," Brett says. "You're pitching. You want to be ready. They were runners-up in the division last year."

"Oh." I still don't look at him.

"Billy Evans's team beat them."

I glance at him. Does he know about the fight? I follow him and start to pitch, but then Mr. Weeks calls us over.

We sit on our bench when the other team takes the field. I had no idea we'd ever have to face Billy's team. Now I remember how he sneered at me the day of the fight. And Sara backing away.

"Where's the girl?" someone yells.

I sit up. The bleachers are full and people spill out onto the sidelines. Mrs. Frazier sits in a lawn chair feeding a bottle to her new baby. David, Mimi and Mom wave from the bleachers. I see Mrs. Post, Mr. Small, my dentist, and Mr. Hyde, the mailman. Kids are everywhere. On bikes. Along the fence in the outfield. In a tree next to the road.

"There's Mr. Carter, from the newspaper," Brett says.

He stands behind the backstop, talking to a man with black hair.

"Who is he talking to?" I ask Brett.

He raises his eyebrows. "Billy's dad. Maybe he's here to check us out. We'll show him."

I feel a little twitch in my stomach. Billy's lucky that his dad cares so much about him and his baseball.

There shouldn't be this many people at league games. I

don't know if they're here to cheer or to complain that I shouldn't be allowed to play. And will they laugh if I pitch badly? Will Mr. Carter write *See, girls shouldn't play baseball?*

No one would make a big deal about a boy's mistake. I push the curls out of my face. I shouldn't be judged differently because I'm a girl.

"Play ball!" the umpire yells. Brett grounds out to first. Doug pops out to the pitcher and Tommy strikes out. Three up, three down. I walk to the mound, sweat trickling down my back.

Brett meets me and tilts his mask so I can see his face.

As I dig my sneaker into the dirt, I feel every inch of my body shaking. I never got nervous like this before our volleyball games last year.

"All right, here we go, Wisconsin. Just throw smoke. No cream puffs."

He goes back to the plate and the first batter steps into the box. He's at least a foot shorter than me, and his baggy pants are held up with a big black belt.

My first pitch sails over Brett's head and crashes into the chain-link fence. I control the next three pitches a little better, but they're all balls. The crowd claps and boos as the kid jogs to first base. I kick the rubber with the toe of my sneaker.

Why am I so tight? I glance up at my mom. I'm too far away to see her face.

I walk the next two batters and now the bases are loaded. Brett and the infielders meet me on the mound. I take off my glove and rub the ball, trying to warm my clammy hands. Someone in the crowd boos.

"If you walk the next batter, you'll walk in a run." Randy crosses his arms.

"No kidding, brilliant observation," Brett says.

"Shut up," Randy says.

"Look, I'm not doing this on purpose," I say.

"Well, maybe you shouldn't be pitching," Randy says.

"Another brilliant statement," Brett says.

"What is your problem?" I say to Randy. He's just like Billy! He shrugs.

"That kid sings in the choir at my church." Doug nods at the boy at the plate. "Last year he got so nervous singing in front of everyone that he puked in the balcony."

We look at him. He stands at the plate, the bat on his shoulders. He's short and skinny, like most of the boys.

"You can do it, Wisconsin," Brett says. Then they head back to their positions.

I stare at the kid at the plate. At least I've never thrown up. I throw. Strike. On my next pitch he pops out to Tommy. Then I strike out the next two batters. Yes! I punch my fist into the pocket of my glove.

It's my turn to bat. I step into the box, swing and miss the first pitch. *Don't try to go for too much.* David's voice is in my head. My hands are clammy, my shoulders tight.

"She's no batter!" the shortstop yells.

The third baseman moves in about five feet. Huh? I scoot my right foot closer to the plate and pull my hips to the left. I only need a hit. With the next pitch I'm still tight but I swing early and manage to hit the ball over the third baseman's head for a single.

By the time the inning is over, we're ahead, three to nothing. I take the mound and concentrate on Brett's mitt.

I don't worry about Randy. I don't look for Mr. Carter. I don't care who watches from the sidelines or from the trees. I no longer hear anyone.

In the end, we win ten to two. As I walk off the field, I feel the muscles in my back loosen. Everyone begins to leave and no one points or yells anything at me.

As we put the equipment away, Mr. Carter walks over to our bench. "Nice pitching, Madison. Why don't you and your mom come to the office on Thursday and we'll talk?"

"What do you want to talk to her about?" Brian asks.

Mr. Carter smiles. "I'm going to write an article about her."

"Whoa!" Tommy says. Little tingles race up my back.

"Okay," I say. Mr. Carter nods and walks off toward the bleachers.

Did Randy hear all that? But he's out on the mound, pitching to Mr. Weeks. He throws and his ball drops into the dirt. He slaps his thigh and readies himself to pitch again. He practiced after our last game, too. Should I?

But then Tommy starts for the bike rack, and I follow. When I look up, I see Sara, Gina and Casey.

"Madison, you're so good," Casey says. "I wouldn't know the first thing to do."

Think of something creative to say! She wears silver hoop earrings and shiny lip gloss. I wish my hair fell into place like that, perfectly feathered. I wish I had earrings like that. I glance down at my sweaty, dirty uniform.

Then I look at Sara. Just two months ago she wrote *best friend* all over my math folder. Last fall we painted our volleyball record, 7–0, on our cheeks and went to school that way. She drops her eyes and covers her stomach with her arms.

One day about a month before school ended she was trying on a plaid skirt her mom had brought home for her. I said, "Why would you want to wear *that*? You look so uncomfortable."

She frowned and folded her arms across her stomach and kept glancing at herself in the mirror, then at me, then back at the mirror. Two days later she wore the skirt to school.

Tommy smiles at Casey the same way he smiled at me.

Casey pulls a box of Tic Tacs from her pocket and tries to open the lid. "Stuck."

She hands the box to Tommy. He opens it and hands it back. What was so hard about that?

"I'd offer you baseball players some but I suppose it would interfere with your tobacco chewing," she says.

"Oh, we don't chew tobacco," Tommy says.

I feel my cheeks burn. Doesn't he know Casey is making fun of us? Sweat streams down my back. The humidity has made my curls stick straight out. If I could, I'd jump out of my body.

"What's that in your ears?" Brett pushes his way into the circle, staring at Casey. "If those hoops were bigger I'd hook a leash to them and pull you around like a dog."

Tommy bursts out laughing. Even Sara and Gina smile.

Casey puts her hands on her hips. "You are so immature, Brett."

"'You are so immature, Brett,'" he sings. "Come on, Wisconsin."

We unlock our bikes and take off through the parking lot. We run stop signs and barrel down hills. When we get to Lake Shore Drive, we slow. Brett goes over each inning, but all I think about was how easily he put down Casey. Why can't I do that?

We dump our bikes in my driveway. We've beaten everyone home.

"I already have my suit on," Brett says.

"Me too."

I look away. Should I go behind the garage to take off my uniform?

"Race you!" Brett says.

We peel off our uniforms and drop them in the grass. We race up the dune, down the steps, across Lake Shore Drive and over the dune and dive into the lake.

The icy water bites into my legs. Ah! We surface and splash each other. Then I point to the sun. It's covered in an orange haze, and we watch it fall behind the trees and houses. The sky is milky white and so thick with humidity that we can't see the lighthouse at Washington Park.

I float. "I love the lake."

"Me too. It's like the ocean because it's so big. Only better because you don't have to worry about sharks and jellyfish."

I nod. It *is* like an ocean, big, blue, stretching for miles and miles. The first time I flew over it, on our way here from Germany, I looked out the window and saw how tiny the whitecaps were below us, how long the shoreline seemed. You could get lost in that lake and never, ever be found again.

The lake still scares me, with its dangerous riptides and powerful waves and the sudden dark blue drop-offs just beyond the sandbars where the water turns noticeably colder. But this is also what I love about it. You just always have to remember to be ready for anything.

Brett is on his back, his arms and legs spread out. His skin is white and freckly.

"Did you know Casey Cunningham when she went to your school?" I ask.

"Yeah, good riddance."

"Why do you say that?"

"I don't see what the big deal is."

"You don't think she's cute?" The question comes out before I can stop myself. I feel as if I can say anything to him.

"She's too mean to be cute."

"How is she mean?" I hold my breath.

"There's this girl, Jenny, who was part of her clique. One day she wore pigtails or something to school and Casey told everyone that Jenny looked like a farmer. She kept laughing at her, and then everyone else laughed. So Jenny was out of the group."

"How do you know this?"

"Everyone knows. You wait. She'll do the same thing at your school."

I begin bouncing, spinning, digging my heel into the hard-packed bottom.

I think about our game and how Randy slapped his thigh on the mound. "Did you see Randy practicing after the game?"

Brett shrugs. "He's the first one there, the last to leave."

"Did he practice like that last year?"

"Nah. I don't think he likes getting shown up by you."

"Does everyone else feel that way?" Like Tommy?

"Nah, cause we don't really have to compete against you. You're on our side."

I nod but I don't get it. Would Randy be as motivated if I were a boy?

"So, Wisconsin. Who taught you to play baseball, your dad?"

"No, my brother. My dad doesn't live with us." I sweep my hands along the top of the water as I twirl.

"Are your parents divorced?"

"Yeah."

It's dark enough that I can't see his face. Then I tell him all about how we left Germany because my mom said my dad was indifferent. I hardly ever talk about this and it feels strange to say that word out loud. *Indifferent.*

But all Brett does is say, "Yeah, well, my parents are divorced, too."

I nod back. Now it just seems as if there's nothing else to say about this.

It's completely dark as we make our way back to my house. Mosquitoes buzz around my ears. The air is thick and still. I stand next to Brett's bike while he puts on his sneakers.

As he swings his leg over his bike, I start to worry about all that I told him. I was practically a baby when we left Germany. It's probably a whole lot easier to be indifferent to a baby than it is a person. If my dad knew me now, would he still be indifferent?

"Don't tell anyone about what I said about my dad, okay?" I ask.

"I can keep a secret. I haven't told anyone about your fight with Billy."

"How do you know about that?"

"Somebody told me the day it happened."

So he's known since the first day of practice. Maybe I *can* trust him.

"I just wish you'd broken his nose," Brett says. "He's a jerk. He thinks he's such a great baseball player."

I watch Brett ride off. He sure doesn't like many people.

"Madison, come in here!" My mom stands at the screen door, frowning.

//

"Where were you?" Mom asks. "Mimi stays with you all day and then goes to your game. You didn't even come over to thank her or say goodbye."

I curl my sandy toes underneath me. My bathing suit is still wet, like a warm glove. I pull my hand through my tangled hair.

"I was so hot. I couldn't stand it. I had to go swimming. It was like I was on fire."

Mom puts her hands on her hips. "I thought the girls were coming over."

"They couldn't." I can't look at her.

"Something is going on. Is everything okay?"

"Yeah."

"Are you sure?"

"What?"

"Usually they're here or you're there or the phone is ringing."

"I was grounded, *remember?*" I begin brushing the sand off my feet. I take great care in getting it out from between my toes.

"Have you had an argument with them?"

"No!" Why can't I tell her?

"Have they said something, maybe, about baseball?" My mom hesitates. "Are you self-conscious?"

"Mom!" Why is she so nosy, having to talk about everything and using corny words like *self-conscious?*

"I'll apologize to Mimi tomorrow. I'm going to bed." I stomp through the door and up the stairs before she can say anything else.

It's so hot the next morning that I wake up early, sweating. To cool off I ride my bike down Lake Shore Drive. The sun has just come up over the lake and haze hangs over the water. I turn off at bus stop 25 and round the corner. I stop in front of Sara's house. The blinds are closed in the kitchen. The Cavanaughs' golf cart sits in the driveway.

One day last summer, when Sara and I were bored at the club pool, we wandered down to the golf clubhouse. Mrs. Cavanaugh and a friend were passing by in the cart.

"Maybe we'll take up golf," Sara said as we jumped into the back.

"Wonderful!" Mrs. Cavanaugh smiled at Mrs. Willis. I

hid my grin. The only reason we were in the cart was because we wanted to drive it.

We watched them tee off on the fifteenth hole, and then Sara begged to drive. Finally Mrs. Cavanaugh agreed. For a while Sara drove slowly and carefully. But at the hill near the seventeenth green, she pushed hard on the accelerator and we roared down the path. Then she turned too sharply and the cart tipped over. We all went flying into a sand trap. The cart was okay and no one got hurt, but Mrs. Cavanaugh was mad about it for weeks.

Now I smile as I stare at Sara's quiet house. I should ring the doorbell. But it's too early. Besides, what if Sara slept over at Casey's last night? Worse yet, if Casey slept over here I'd be so embarrassed, standing at the door with nothing to say. I turn around and ride home.

David, Mom and Mimi are at the table. I pour a glass of orange juice and stand at the counter.

"Where have you been so early?" Mom asks. "I was looking for you."

"Bike riding."

She wrinkles her forehead and looks at me. I stare back. Then I smile at Mimi. "I'm sorry I took off last night before saying goodbye. I was just so hot."

Mimi nods. "You played a fine game."

"Thanks. And thanks for coming, too."

"You got a call this morning," Mom says. I stand up straight. Sara? "Mike Carter wants to confirm that I'm bringing you in on Thursday morning for an interview."

David lowers the paper. "Wow. He really knows his baseball, Mad."

"He said he talked to you about this last night." Mom shakes her damp hair out of her face. "But I'm just not sure this is necessary."

Necessary? "I can do it. It's not a big deal."

"It's not a matter of whether you can do something or not. I just worry about adding more pressure on you."

"Maddie can take it." David doesn't look up from the paper. "Nothing fazes her."

Right. Nothing fazes me. But . . . I'm nervous before games. I lean into the counter.

Mom shakes her head. "I don't know. And I have a meeting Thursday morning."

"Oh, come on." David drops the paper on the table. "It's not a big deal. He'll ask her a bunch of questions and she'll jabber on like always. It'll be easy."

"I don't jabber." I put my hands on my hips.

"Well," Mimi says to Mom, "maybe you could change your meeting."

Mom raises her eyebrows and looks at me.

I think about dramatic pauses and not saying anything stupid, and a twitch tingles up my back. I want her to come. But she can't say anything about feminism or being the only woman on law review. "If you promise not to say anything."

She nods. "I'll see what I can do."

After lunch I see Huey sitting on Crystal's back stoop. The weeds and grass in Crystal's yard still stand shin high.

"What's going on?" Huey wears his leather pants and

David's striped T-shirt. He squints up at me, lines wrinkled across his forehead.

"Nothing. I just had lunch."

He nods, then scrunches his eyebrows. "Isn't it a little early for lunch?"

"It's twelve-thirty."

"Oh." He shakes his head as if water is stuck in his ear and he can't get it out. I frown. He must have just woken up. My mom would have a fit if I slept this late.

"When are you going to mow the lawn?" I ask.

Huey shrugs. "I haven't mowed a yard since I was a kid."

"It's easy. You put in some gas, pull the cord, and there you go."

What does he do all day, anyway?

"It'll be tough with this deep grass." He squints up at me. "Want to help?"

"I have baseball practice."

Huey pulls the newspaper out from underneath him and opens to the sports section. "You gave up only three hits. Impressive." He grins. "We've got a little trendsetter here. Pushing buttons, so to speak."

"I'm playing because I *like* it."

"Okay. Okay. What do the boys think about this?"

"They don't care." I stare at the pine tree. "That reporter wants to interview me tomorrow."

"Uh-oh. Reporters. They'll coax you out and then throw you to the wolves." He chuckles.

I can't imagine Mr. Carter throwing me to anything. But then I'm not sure. "I need to have a lot of dramatic pauses, right?"

"Listen. After each question, pause at least seven seconds, like you're thinking. Then answer, but don't elaborate. Don't reveal too much. Be careful of trick questions, like 'What do you want to be when you grow up?' They ask those questions to see what motivates you. If you say something like 'I want to be remembered as a great songwriter,' they'll call you, I don't know, a has-been or self-absorbed or something."

"Delusional," I say, remembering the *Rolling Stone* article.

"Yeah. Delusional." Huey stands. "Good luck."

"What about the lawn?"

"I'll get to it. You'll see."

12

"Look what I brought," I say to Brett.

I put my bike in the rack and open my backpack. Brett grins and takes out a plump water balloon. We fill our gloves and walk to the field. Mr. Weeks is still in the parking lot, digging through his trunk. Everyone else stands around, too hot to move.

"Randy, catch," Brett says. But Randy doesn't get his hands up in time and the balloon explodes at his feet, soaking him. He stands there, mouth open, frowning.

"I want one!" Doug yells. I toss one to him, then Tommy. Pretty soon everyone is laughing and throwing them at each other. A balloon breaks against my back, warm water soaking my shirt. Brett grins at me, and I raise my arm to throw one at him.

"Whoa!" Mr. Weeks jogs to the field. "What's going on here?"

"Madison brought water balloons," Brian says.

"That's enough." Mr. Weeks glances at me.

Brett squats, putting on his shin guards. I throw a balloon in front of him and water sprays over him. Everyone laughs, Randy the loudest.

"Madison," Mr. Weeks says, but he's grinning.

"Sorry," I say. And we all crack up.

Later, after batting practice, the infielders are at their bases. Brett is behind the plate. The stands are empty. I rear back and throw. *Aahh.* What a great feeling! The ball explodes into Brett's mitt. He falls and stays there, spread out in the dirt.

"Killed by a speeding bullet! That was awesome, Wisconsin."

Everyone laughs. Practice is nearly over, but I could stay here all day, throwing, hitting, laughing. I glance around the infield.

How different everything is now compared to our first practice. *Just give her a chance.* Whose dad said that? It doesn't matter, because most of the boys seem glad I'm here. Just a while ago, Doug said to me, "You're the best player we've ever had." But he made sure to say it when Randy wasn't around.

"Thanks, you're pretty good yourself," I said. "The home run king." He's in a bit of a hitting slump now, but no one else has hit a home run so far. If we're going to keep winning, it'll be because of all of us.

Donny stands in the batter's box. He's the youngest, and

usually he doesn't leave Randy's side. His T-shirt hangs to his knees and even the smallest helmet swims on his head. Every time he swings, he raises his left foot so his weight falls backward. When he swings he either misses the ball or hits it straight up.

I throw again, and Donny swings and misses. He heaves his bat at the backstop and buries his face in the bend of his arm. Brett takes off his mask and is about to say something to Donny—something mean, I can tell—when I mouth, "No!"

"Don't tell me to use a lighter bat," Donny whispers through his arm when I walk to the plate. "I tried that. It doesn't work. Go get Randy."

I glance at Randy, who stands at third base.

"You keep lifting your left leg so your weight goes backward," I say.

"No, I don't."

I lay my glove across Donny's left foot. "Don't move it when you swing." David taught me this; I used to move my foot, too. I go back to the mound and throw a pitch. As Donny swings and misses, his foot rises and knocks off the glove. He looks down at his feet, then at me.

He puts the glove back across his foot and crouches. He continues to lift his foot and knock off the glove. But by the end of his turn, he's figured out how to stop himself. Now his weight goes forward. He even hits a couple of pitches.

"Thanks, Madison," Donny says as he hurries by me to the outfield. This is the first time he's ever said my name.

I smile. "Sure."

We take a break and sit under the tree. Donny scoots across the grass and sits next to me. Brett is on the other side. Tommy is by himself, up against the tree. Randy sits across from me, his arms crossed, his cap pulled over his eyebrows.

"Johnson Electric is the only other undefeated team," Mr. Weeks says. "Both of us could go the season undefeated. If that's the case, we'll play them and the winner will be Long Beach champs. But anything could happen."

"That's Billy Evans's team," Brett says to me. "They play at Abbott field."

"Billy Evans says he's going to bean you," Donny says. Everyone looks at me.

"Now, Donny, no one is going to bean anyone," Mr. Weeks says.

"Billy is. That's what he's telling everyone. He's going to bean Madison in the head." He turns to me. "You should know."

Bean me. Throw a pitch to hit me. Hurt me.

"No one is going to intentionally hit anyone," Mr. Weeks says. "Or there will be serious consequences. Someone could get really hurt."

Randy snorts. Everyone looks at him.

"What's so funny?" I throw back my shoulders. So does Randy.

"If you're gonna play, you have to deal with the bad stuff that goes with it." Randy shrugs.

"I don't know what you mean by bad stuff, Randy,"

Mr. Weeks says. "But no one should have to deal with getting intentionally hit. Now, what's going on here?"

He looks at Randy, then me. He glances at the others, but no one says anything.

I should tell him how Randy tried to get the others to go against me. And how he sneers at me when he says I better not make any errors.

"Madison, is anyone giving you a hard time?" Mr. Weeks asks.

"Yes." I look around. Randy's eyes widen. "Brett is. The other day he said my slide looked like a belly flop."

Everyone starts laughing, even Randy.

Mr. Weeks shakes his head, smiling.

Belly flop! Every ten minutes for the rest of practice someone yells this out. We laugh, but I keep thinking about Billy. Maybe I'll throw a pitch close to his body, brush him off the plate. Make him nervous. Then I'll bean *him* right in his chest.

But I remember how hard his fist came back at me that day. What if he hits me in the nose again? Or in the middle of the *o*? Getting beaned will hurt. And it will be right in front of all those people at the game.

After practice, Randy goes back on the field and pitches to Mr. Weeks. Brett and I walk to the bike rack. Tommy comes up and hangs his glove on his bike's gearshift.

"Your bike is great," I say.

"Yeah, I know." Tommy swings his leg over it.

Is his bike the only thing we'll ever talk about?

"It's fast, too," he says.

"I have to go to the orthodontist," Brett says.

"Did you get it for your birthday?" I take off my hat. Do I have dirt on my face?

"My bike is really fast." Brett says. He stands with his back to Tommy, which is very rude. I decide not to look at him.

"Did I get what?" Tommy asks.

"Your bike."

"My birthday is in February."

"So this wasn't a present?"

"From who?"

"What?" I tilt my head. Brett snickers and I shoot him a dirty look.

"I can't go swimming today," Brett says. "I have to go to the orthodontist."

"Fine," I say. "Then *go*."

Brett steps back. That wasn't nice, but I want to talk to Tommy. What's wrong with that?

Brett rides off, and I turn back to Tommy. He's smiling at his bike.

"No one can beat me," he says. "I raced all morning with my brothers."

"Oh."

"The gears on my old bike used to slip, especially in fifth gear."

His skin is brown from the sun and his eyes are blue.

At least I'm not here in my uniform. I begin twisting my handlebars. Does he still have a girlfriend?

"My bike slips in fourth gear." Although not if I oil and tighten the chain.

"That's easy to fix." Tommy squats and looks at my

111

bike. "But I have to have a wrench. I'm really good at fixing things."

I am, too. I don't know why I don't tell him this.

Randy walks up and looks at us. He's almost smiling. Is he glad I didn't tell on him? Something feels different.

The two of them ride off down the street.

Riding home, I slow as I pass Crystal's house. Huey still hasn't cut the grass. But I have other things to think about. Like Tommy.

The next night after dinner David says, "Let's go to the middle-league game at the high school."

We climb into Mom's car. "I want you to meet Ross Taylor. He coaches a middle-league team."

"Why?" Middle league is for players when they turn thirteen.

David pulls into the street. We pass Mrs. Minor, who's watering her lawn as she talks to Crystal.

"He said he'd draft you for next year," David says.

"*Draft me?* I'm not playing middle league next year."

"Why not?"

"I don't know."

"You're the best player in your league. In the whole town! You'll be great."

"Middle league is a lot different." The season is longer and teams travel to other towns to play. The boys are older. Most of the pitchers throw curveballs.

"Just see what you think," David says.

At the field, we stand behind one of the benches. There

are only a dozen people watching. I remember the pitcher from school. He's only two years older, but he's a lot taller than me, and he has a faint mustache. He used to be short and skinny, but now his arms are long, his hands huge. Like Randy.

Mimi always says about David, "He hasn't come into his body yet." Well, these guys have. And when the guys from my team get here, most of them will have grown, too. It won't be long until they're all taller and stronger than me.

The pitcher winds up, his motion wild and jerky, but the ball zings across the plate twice as fast as anything I've ever thrown.

The boy at the plate swings and misses. He steps out of the box and adjusts his batting glove. He knocks the dirt out of his cleats. In our league, everyone wears sneakers. No one has mustaches or batting gloves or pitches this fast.

The pitcher throws again. This time the ball flies over the catcher's head and into the fence. Could Brett catch this guy? I flinch, remembering our conversation. *Then go,* I said to him. Is he mad at me?

"What's wrong with the pitcher's motion?" David asks. "Watch what happens when he kicks his left leg."

I watch the pitcher raise his arms above his head, turn on the rubber and lift his leg. His knee kicks nearly level with his forehead before he brings it down with the pitch. The boy at the plate swings and hits a foul ball over our heads.

"It's too high or something."

"Right," David says. "It gives him power, but he'll run

into trouble later. It slows his motion toward home. Runners will steal on him. Come on, Madison, watch him."

The pitcher winds up and throws. His ball whizzes across the plate and hits the batter in the arm. The boy yells and falls, and the umpire stops the game. A parent helps the boy stand, and he hobbles off the field, cradling his arm.

I squeeze my hands into fists. Is his arm broken?

After a few minutes the boy walks off to one of the cars. Is he on his way to the hospital? I glance at David, but he watches the game.

In the fourth inning, Ross Taylor comes over and says hello. He's tall and young, with long black hair. He wears mirror aviator sunglasses, and I can't see his eyes.

He points to the pitcher. "I taught Tim how to throw a curveball this year. Do you know how to throw a curveball yet?"

"No." Because my brother thinks I'm too young. David looks at me with his lips pinched closed. And I decide not to tell this to Ross. "Is that boy's arm broken?"

"Hope not," Ross says. "He's on his way to the hospital." We turn when the umpire calls an out at the plate. The teams trade sides.

"Gotta go. You know, I can make sure you're on my team next year," he calls over his shoulder as he walks off.

I nod and drop my eyes.

Back in the car David says, "What do you think?" He turns onto Lake Shore Drive. A hot, humid, milky haze hangs over the lake below us.

I shift in my seat. "I bet it's broken."

"That kid's arm? Maddie, he didn't get out of the way."

"They don't pitch like that in the town league." Although I haven't faced Billy yet. Will I be able to get out of the way if he tries to bean me?

"You have so much natural talent." David shakes his head. "I mean, look at you! You should be excited about how good you are. Aren't you having a blast playing?"

"I like practices." And Tommy. And even Brett. Yesterday I loved the feeling of throwing my hardest and hitting Brett's mitt every time.

"Think about what Ross said. I know you could do it."

Is he even listening to me?

Besides, how can he be so sure? Right now I'm bigger and stronger than most boys my age. But what will happen when they catch up? I don't want to get hurt or make any errors. And I don't always want to be the only girl out there.

David drops me off at home and then drives to meet his friends. I get out and watch as the car climbs the hill. David's an okay brother. No, a really good brother. But I won't play middle league next year just because he wants me to do it. Why does he have to push me so much?

I'm in my room when I hear the doorbell. Mom puts her head inside my door. "Someone's here for you. A boy from your team."

Brett! Maybe he's not mad at me after all. I run down the stairs.

Tommy smiles at me from the living room and a blush stings my cheeks. How did he know where I live?

He holds up a wrench. "I came to fix your bike."

"Thanks! That's . . . so nice of you." We go outside and I open the garage door.

"Whoa, where'd you get all this stuff?" He picks up a long piece of driftwood and slices it through the air like a sword.

"My mom can't throw anything away." I wheel my bike into the driveway.

Tommy turns it upside down, tightens the chain and then spins the wheels.

"It looks okay now," he says. "Maybe it's slipping gears because you're not doing it right. You have to pedal when you change gears."

"I know that." I know how to change gears. I know everything about my bike.

"Well, okay." He turns my bike over.

We walk to the front and sit on the porch. I sneak peeks at him. He wears new white Adidas tennis shoes. His legs are tan. I bring my knees to my chest and fold my arms over them, hiding my scars.

"Want a pop?" I ask.

"No, thanks."

I've hung around boys all my life, and I've never had trouble talking before. I wish being with Tommy were as easy as, well, being with Brett. My shoulders sink into my knees. Tomorrow I'll apologize to him for what I said.

I straighten. "Want to go swimming?"

"Swimming? Now? You mean, in the lake?"

I nod.

"I heard Chicago opened up the sewer locks and all these dead fish are gonna wash up onshore," he says. "Like a couple years ago. Doesn't that gross you out?"

Of course it grosses me out. All those poor dead fish on the sand. But Mimi and I listened to the Chicago jazz station this morning and I didn't hear anything about this.

"I was swimming yesterday, and I didn't see any fish."

"Well, it's pretty cold still, huh?"

"No!" How can he not want to swim in the lake? Sara would laugh if she heard him say this. I dig a hole in the sand with my toe. Mosquitoes buzz around my ears as a voice booms in my head: *Say something!* "Does Randy know you came over here?"

Tommy shakes his head. "No! And don't tell him."

"Why not?"

"He doesn't really like that you're playing."

"Why?"

"He thinks girls will drag everyone down. You know, make it no fun."

"What do you think?"

"About what?"

"About me playing!"

"You're a really good pitcher." He leans into me until our shoulders touch. He smells fresh, like laundry detergent. "I gotta go."

I don't want him to leave. "Thanks for fixing my bike. That was nice." Although I'm not sure anything was really wrong with it.

He smiles as he climbs onto his bike. Then he waves and disappears up the hill.

He likes me. I think.

I take a deep breath. I no longer smell him, but just the thought of him sends cool tingles up and down my arms.

13

Mom and I sit facing Mr. Carter at his desk at the *News-Dispatch* office. I try to see what he's writing in his notebook but it's upside down.

"Were you nervous about signing up?" Mr. Carter asks.

So far he's asked me, "How old are you? Where do you go to school? What other sports do you play? How do you see the ball so well?" But this question feels different. *Don't elaborate* Huey told me.

I count to seven. "Kind of."

"What were you kind of nervous about?" He keeps writing.

I glance at Mom but she just smiles. I don't want everyone in Long Beach to know I was worried about what my friends would say or how I'd look in my uniform or whether I'd make a mistake. I especially don't want Mom to know.

"Mom, any thoughts?" Mr. Carter looks at her.

"I think she was perhaps a bit worried about being stigmatized as a trailblazer."

I whip my head to look at her. Stigmatized? Trailblazer?

"No!" I'm so angry I can't look at her. I watch Mr. Carter write in his notebook.

"You *are* a trailblazer, you know," he says. "I bet in a couple years we'll have a girls' softball league in town. You've paved the way. What do you think about that?"

This time I count to twenty. I shift around in my seat. I feel Mom's eyes on me, but I don't look. Why did I ask her to come, anyway? Why does she have to wear that wrinkly shirt?

But then something else makes me angry. Can't girls have a baseball league? Can't we just play with the boys? Finally I say, "Girls won't do anything just because of me."

"So modest!" He stands and shakes my hand, then Mom's. "Thanks for coming in. And good luck. I'll be watching. You're quite a young lady. Oh, one more thing. Is there anything you hope or wish for? You know, for the future?"

The trick question! I can't tell him about wanting Tommy to like me or wishing for a new bike. I can't be too revealing. I glance at a newspaper on the end of his desk. The hostages. That's it. "What I really want is for the hostages to be rescued."

Mr. Carter pauses. "Well, that's not quite what I was expecting. Isn't that something? A baseball player with a social conscience."

"A what?"

"That's very thoughtful of you."

I nod, although I'm still not sure what he means. "Thank you."

Outside, I unlock my bike from the telephone pole. Mom stands next to me. She has to go back to her office for a meeting, and I'm going home. But she doesn't move. "What did you think?"

"Why did you have to say that about me?"

"Madison, he asked what I thought, so I told him. I'm sorry if I embarrassed you."

"You said you wouldn't say anything."

"I was trying to be helpful and honest. I didn't mean— Oh, I'm sorry, honey. I shouldn't have said anything. But I'm wondering about all this. Can we talk about it? Why the idea of trailblazing bothers you?"

"Because I'm not like that."

"But you *are* the only girl, and I know how that feels. When I was on law review I felt like I had to be perfect or the men would say I didn't deserve to be there."

"This is different!"

"Well, yes, but . . . When I was in school—"

I cut her off. "I don't want to hear about it! I'm not *like* you."

She sucks in her cheeks and wrinkles her forehead. When I get on my bike, I'm going to ride as fast as I can. Faster than I've ever ridden.

"Okay, fair enough. But we're going to talk about this tonight at home."

With that I take off down the street, standing on my pedals as I pump.

* * *

"How did it go?" David asks at dinner. I stare at my plate. This is the second time this week we've had eggs for dinner because Mom couldn't get to the grocery store.

I glance at her. She's been home for an hour, but I just now came out of my room. I hurt her feelings with what I said this afternoon, but if I apologize, we'll have to talk about it. I reach to twirl my mood ring. Of course, it's gone. If only Sara would call.

"He wanted to know about how I learned to play, where I go to school, what kinds of other things I like to do."

"Jeez, did you give him your entire life story?" David laughs. But it's not a funny ha-ha laugh.

I glare at him. "I didn't reveal too much. I had lots of dramatic pauses."

They both look at me.

"What are you talking about?" David asks.

I don't like the way David is talking to me. "Huey said reporters ask trick questions and want to throw you to the wolves if you're not careful. He told me not to reveal too much."

"I guess he would know," Mom says.

"You mean Huey is still here?" David sits back in his chair. "You talked to him?"

"Yeah, I talk to him all the time. He has writer's block. And he and Crystal are a couple now." I throw back my shoulders and tip back in my chair. *There are just some things in this world I know and you don't*, I tell David with my eyes.

122

"What about his wife?" David asks.

I drop my chair back down. I've read the *Rolling Stone* article about him at least twenty times and it never mentions a wife. "He's not married."

"I read somewhere he got married a couple years ago," David says.

"What else do you and Huey talk about?" Mom asks.

"The weather. Baseball. Crystal's lawn. We talk on the front stoop."

I stare at the little silver peace sign that hangs from her neck. Sara's mom wears pearls, even when she plays golf.

"You just show up on the doorstep?" David asks.

I nod and push my plate away. "He never told me he's married."

How long has Huey been gone from his wife and kids? A month? A year? Do they know where he is? Why did he leave? What if his kids have turned out to be really interesting and nice, only he doesn't know this because he left?

But . . . Huey is so cool. What if something is wrong with his family and he *had* to leave? Maybe the kids cried all the time. Maybe his wife didn't want to follow him around to his concerts. Or maybe he just didn't like them.

I glance at Mom. What if her story about Dad being indifferent isn't the whole truth? What if we *made* him that way? Maybe this is our fault. Or hers.

I sit up and lean across the table. "I cried a lot when I was a baby, right?"

Mom looks at me. "You were pretty colicky for the first

123

three months. But I've told you about that, remember? How the only thing that settled you down was walking by that little lake near where we lived?"

I nod. "Did Dad ever walk me by the lake?"

"No. He left on duty for six months right after you were born."

"I wasn't colicky," David says.

I stare at Mom. "Did it make Dad mad when you said you wanted to come back here and go to law school?"

Mom pauses. "No, he didn't really care what we did. But I think you're trying to get at something else here. What is it?"

I snort and cross my arms and sit back. She always turns my questions into questions of her own. *Just answer me!* My heart starts to pound. "I don't see why you have to work all the time."

"I love what I do. I love helping people who otherwise wouldn't be able to afford a lawyer. I feel like I'm contributing to society."

I roll my eyes.

"Why does that bother you?" she asks. I shrug. "You rolled your eyes, so it must. I feel fortunate to be able to do what I do. Most women never get these opportunities."

I hold up my hands. I don't want to hear about it.

"How else would we live, Madison?" she asks.

"Dad sends money, right?" David asks.

Mom nods. "Once in a while. I put it away for college. I could take him to court but I just never wanted to. Besides, aren't we doing okay here on our own?"

David shrugs and takes a bite of his eggs. I can feel

Mom's eyes on me, but I won't look at her. What if this is her fault, not Dad's?

But then I see how she's looking at me, her eyes soft. And I feel this space widening between us, like what happens when you're in the lake and you don't hang on to each other's rafts.

14

On Tuesday there's a threat of rain, so I ride to the game with Mimi and David. Cars line both sides of the street near the field. Dozens of people stand at the fence. I see Mrs. Post and the neighbors. Artie and D.J. wave from behind the bench. Ross Taylor, the middle-league coach, stands in the top row of the bleachers.

My heart shoots up into my throat.

"You're going to have a big crowd again." David turns to me.

"They're not just coming to see me."

"They're coming to see who, the right fielder?"

"You're making me nervous."

"How can you be nervous?" David asks. "You're the best player out there."

Mimi pulls to the curb.

"What does that have to do with anything?" I put my hand in David's glove. The leather feels cold and stiff. With my other hand I trace his name along the thumb.

"You go and do your best," Mimi says. "Don't worry about a thing."

She winks. I sigh and get out.

"Don't forget to push off with your whole foot," David yells as I walk away.

I tug on my swimsuit and run my hand down the front of my shirt. The other team is warming up. I sit next to Brett on our bench. I try not to look at the crowd.

"Hey." I watch him put on his shin guards. Dirt smudges his cheeks, and a big cowlick on the front of his head makes a handful of red hair point toward the sky. "Want to go swimming later?"

Brett shrugs but doesn't look at me.

"I know Randy's pitching tonight, but let's warm up until he's ready."

"Okay." He raises his eyebrows. "Your shoulder okay?"

"Yeah. I just wish there weren't so many people here."

"Ah, who cares?" He grins.

I smile back. We're okay. We walk to the outfield along the foul line and begin throwing. Two boys on banana-seat bikes hang over the fence, watching.

The ball feels hard and small as I aim at Brett's mitt. I throw and it lands right where I aim.

"Look at the girl," says a boy on the banana-seat bike. He and his friend are about our age, but I don't know them. "Hey, you throw like a boy."

"Maybe you *are* a boy," the other says, sitting on his bike and holding the top of the fence. "You sure don't look like a girl."

I throw the ball as hard as I can at the fence, aiming just below where he's holding on. He lets go as the ball smacks into the chain links, loses his balance and falls into the grass. His friend cracks up.

"Shut up!" The boy picks himself up, gets back on his bike and pulls away. His friend follows, still laughing.

"You showed him." Brett squats and holds out his mitt. "Let's go, Wisconsin."

But I can't move. I don't look like a girl? All this time I've been certain everyone was laughing at how my breasts look under the uniform. And my hair. I never imagined anyone might mistake me for a boy.

Mr. Weeks calls to us. I stand with the others, my head down. I like being a girl. I don't want people to think I'm a boy.

"Play ball!" the umpire yells.

I walk to third base.

"Go, Madison!" someone yells from the crowd.

I search all those faces staring at me from the bleachers. There are even more people here than last time. Brian tosses a grounder to me, and I scoop it up and throw it back. But the ball sails way to the right and into the fence.

"She throws like a girl!" someone yells from the crowd. A group behind the other team's bench starts to laugh.

I kick the dirt with my toe. When I make a mistake, someone says I throw like a girl. But when I strike a batter out, do they say I pitch like a boy?

My muscles are thick and tense and my hands shake. I don't have this fear when I play volleyball. Maybe that's because no one comes to our games. And no one yells at me from the stands. And because I play with only girls.

"Let's go, Madison!" someone else yells.

I look up and see Sara, her arms folded. She stands apart from the others and watches me. I want to run over and tell her about that kid who said I look like a boy. She'll laugh and say what a jerk and everything will be back to normal.

"Batter up!" The umpire dusts off the plate. Randy glances around the infield, his eyes resting on me. Lately, he's been okay. At least not mean.

He turns to the plate and throws. Strike. He throws again and the batter swings too late and misses. Strike two. If Randy could keep pitching like this, he'd be un-stoppable.

He winds up and throws, his motion smooth. Strike three. He always keeps his arm extended, high over his head. It's hard to do, but it'll give him more power. That's what David says.

He strikes out the next batter on three pitches. I feel a twitch in my stomach. Randy has a perfect motion and he can already throw a curve. All I have is a fastball. It's fast and consistent, more than anyone else's I've seen so far in the league, but eventually these boys will figure out how to hit it.

The next batter hits a soft grounder up the line toward me. I scoop up the ball and fire to first. Three outs.

When we're up, Brett singles, Doug walks, then Tommy

strikes out. My turn: I stand in the box and stare at the pitcher. He throws, I swing and miss. Someone yells, "She should go home to her dolls!"

Someone else boos. I don't play with dolls. Even if I did, so what? I can do both. In the bleachers, Mom watches me, her palm against her cheek. Then I smack the end of my bat on the plate.

Don't look at the crowd or Sara or Tommy. I swing at the next pitch. It sails over the shortstop's head. I stop on first and turn. Brett scores, and we're up one to nothing.

I score when Brian hits a double. I score again in the third. I field a couple of grounders but none are hit very hard. By the last inning we're up five to zero.

The gray clouds pass and the last of the evening sun blazes over the trees. The air is muggy, and I feel the sweat glue my swimsuit to my body. I bend over, waiting for Randy's pitch. The batter swings and the ball comes at me hard, bouncing once, twice. Move! But it's so fast. If it takes a bad bounce, it could hit me in the face.

I reach down and across my body and stop the ball with a backhand catch. I throw to first just in time. The crowd cheers. I take a deep breath. That was too close. Then the next batter pops out to Brian, and Randy strikes out the last batter. We win.

We shake hands with the other team. Doug brings up the rear, his arms folded, his head down. He was great in the infield but got thrown out at home. He also struck out twice. In practice, he hits balls all over the field.

"You'll get it back," I say to him.

He shrugs and looks away.

Mr. Weeks motions me to follow him back out to the field. We stop at third base. "You had some nice plays tonight. But remember to move side to side and field the ball between your legs. Use your body, if you need to. Backhanding the ball works if there's nothing else you can do. But it isn't a high-percentage play."

"Oh, okay." I know this. I can't tell him I'm afraid. "Thanks."

I walk off the field. As Brett puts away the catching equipment, Tommy walks his bike over to me. I take off my cap and sweat drips down my cheeks. "Want to go to the Dairy Queen?"

I'm so surprised that my mouth almost drops open. "But I don't have my bike."

"You could ride on my seat and hang on to me. I'll pedal."

I have grass stains on my knees and sweat stains across my stomach. What if we run into those boys who said I looked like a boy? I'd die if they said anything to me in front of Tommy.

He swings his leg over his bike. Does he like me? What if we run into my friends? I imagine holding Tommy's waist and laughing at something he said. Then seeing Casey and Sara. They'd be so jealous!

I turn to the field. Brett puts the extra balls in the duffel bag.

"So are you coming, or what?" Tommy asks.

I can tell Brett I forgot about swimming. Or I had an emergency. Still, I don't move. Something about how

Tommy said *or what* bothers me. Or maybe it's the memory of sitting on the porch next to him with nothing to say.

That could happen at the Dairy Queen.

"I just remembered I have to go. I'm meeting my friends." I wince.

Tommy shrugs and pulls away. "Okay, see you."

As he rides off, I feel a sting in my heart. I should have gone!

"Ready?" Brett comes up behind me. I say goodbye to my family and hand David my hat and glove. Then I climb on the back of Brett's bike.

We ride past people who are walking away from the field. Someone yells, "Great game, Madison!" I wave. The wind feels warm but nice against my hot cheeks. I hold on to Brett's belt as he goes over each inning.

"Then in the third you hit that line drive and drove me in, and I knew we'd win."

When Brett turns the corner, I nearly slide off. I grab his waist. He feels strong and I hold on tight.

At a stoplight, Sara, Gina and Casey wait, too.

For a moment I watch them, undetected. They're dressed in cutoffs, T-shirts and flip-flops. Their toenails are painted the same color red and they carry purses.

Gina parts her hair down the middle and it feathers to the sides, like Casey's. But Sara's hair waves in all directions. Just like mine.

We always laughed about that, even looked forward to how crazy our hair could get. Like on Saturday mornings, after sleeping over together, when we'd stand at the mirror and compare our heads.

All of a sudden I'm sick of thinking about hair and clothes.

My mom and her friends don't care. Last summer Susan and two of Mom's other friends from college visited for the weekend. They spent the whole time in shorts and old T-shirts, hair messy, no makeup, laughing while they drank coffee and talked on the porch. They had so much fun. I sat off to the side, quiet, listening, watching.

Now the girls see me. If only I were on the back of Tommy's bike! I stare at the light. Come on, *change*.

When the light turns, I take one last look. Sara stands with her arms folded again. Our eyes hold and she opens her mouth as if to say something. But I look away.

Soon we're sailing down Lake Shore Drive. At bus stop 28 Brett carries his bike down the wooden stairs and drops it in the sand. We take off our uniforms, race past the lifeguard and swim to the sandbar.

We try to catch minnows in our hands until it's too dark to see. Then we float on our backs and search for the first star.

What did Sara want to say to me?

"Those were my friends with Casey," I say.

"Why didn't you talk to them?"

I stand. My body is numb from the cold water. "They left me at the fight I had with Billy. Casey made them do it." There, I said it out loud.

"Really?"

I nod. But there's something about this that doesn't feel right. I dive under the water, where it's dark and freezing, and swim toward shore.

Brett follows. On the beach he picks up his bike and we climb the stairs. We say goodbye and I start down the hill, my uniform and shoes in my hands. I stop under the street-light in front of Crystal's. Weeds still grow in the garage doorway and the grass is shin deep in the yard. What's with Huey?

I open the back door to find Mom at the kitchen table, staring at me.

15

I lower myself into a chair, my uniform clutched to my chest.

But then she sits back and pulls her hand through her curls. "Please tell me what's going on with you. You seem so angry with me. And you aren't speaking to Sara. Something happened, Madison. I can tell."

"I don't know. We just aren't talking."

"Did you have an argument?"

I shrug. She leans forward, her elbows on the table. Her eyes don't flit around, worrying about the work she has to do. She wants to understand. I take a breath. "Sara told everyone about baseball before I even made up my mind to do it. And she backed up and abandoned me at the fight with Billy."

"Abandoned you?"

I nod.

"You and Sara have been friends for a long time. Why would she abandon you?"

I wince. Isn't it obvious? Casey turned her against me. Sara doesn't want to be friends with anyone who has fist-fights with boys. Can't Mom see this?

"How were things with Sara before the fight?"

"Fine!" Too many questions!

The fight is the problem. And Casey. Or maybe both. But now I remember: *I don't care what you do!* I yelled at Sara when she told me she might not play volleyball next year. I yelled at her again when she said she wouldn't wear her football jersey anymore. And the day she and Gina came to school with matching red nail polish I said their nails looked stupid and stomped off.

Maybe this is my fault because I'm not enough like a girl.

I want to crawl under the table and never come out.

"How do you know she told everyone about baseball?"

"Because Casey teased me about it in front of everyone, and Sara was the only one who knew and she had such a guilty look on her face."

"Have you two talked about this? Maybe there's an explanation."

"There's no explanation!" But maybe . . . I ran from the bathroom that day. And then I threw my mood ring at Sara. I twist my bare finger. My mom glances at it.

I'm so angry but I don't know who I'm angry with. Sara? Casey? Mom? Me?

"Why do you have to ask so many questions?"

"Because I love you and I want to understand what's happening to you."

"Well, you wouldn't understand."

"I understand the pressure you're under. And all this attention. I've been there."

"Yeah, but you loved it."

"Not all the time. I want you to be happy, Madison."

"Well, we should have more money so you wouldn't have to work all the time and you could buy some real clothes. That would make me happy."

She scrunches her forehead. "What's wrong with my clothes?"

I roll my eyes and look away. I'm cold; my arms and legs are shaking.

"This is the second time you've brought up my job," she says. "Do you feel like I'm not spending enough time at home with you?"

"Oh, *God*, Mom."

She covers her mouth with her hand. Are there tears in her eyes? I didn't mean to make her cry. What's the matter with me?

"Maybe I can be home more."

"That's not it," I say.

"What is it?" She puts her hand on top of mine. This is so sudden and familiar that I want to climb into her lap and put my face into that soft part of her neck. But then I'm horrified. I'm not a baby. How can I even *think* of doing this?

I charge up the stairs and throw open the screen in my

window. The wind blows hot, dry air over the pine trees. I listen for the lake, but all I hear is a door banging against a house somewhere. Then voices. Crystal and Huey stand under the streetlight.

Crystal is talking and waving her arms, angry. I climb onto the roof, but I'm too far to hear. No stars are out and I barely make out the TV tower. I'll have to stay.

Crystal wraps her arms around herself and shakes Huey off when he touches her shoulder. He leans against the streetlight. The light frames them, like a spotlight.

Maybe Huey just told her about his wife.

Crystal's hair hangs in her face and her shoulders sag. The last time I saw Crystal under the streetlight like this was when the snow buried her bare feet and swirled around her shins. Her thin arms reached out in front of her, as if trying to catch something. Around and around she ran.

Huey reaches for her and hugs her, and Crystal buries her head in his chest. Now they're okay. But something else catches my eye, something green flashes in Mrs. Minor's garage. Then the garage lights snap off.

Later, when I lie in bed I realize that Mrs. Minor—dressed in her lime-green housecoat—was in her garage watching Huey and Crystal, too.

The next morning I stay in bed until I hear Mimi's voice and then Mom's car. Finally I come down the stairs.

"You slept late," Mimi says when I sit at the table. "Your mom couldn't wait. She had to be in court."

She kisses me on the forehead. She smells like soap and flowers. I smile.

"How about an egg pop?" Mimi asks.

"Sure."

An egg pop is a fried egg laid across a piece of toast smothered in butter and jelly. It's delicious and reminds me of winter vacation mornings when Mimi stayed with us.

"Something in the paper," Mimi says. "On the front page."

"Have the hostages been rescued?"

I flip over the paper. And there I am, across two columns. My arm is back and my leg is reared up. My brows are together and my mouth is closed. And my left arm is across my chest, hiding my breasts.

Underneath the picture the headline reads, *Superstar with a Social Conscience Takes On Boys*. The article by Mr. Carter fills the whole lower right side of the paper. I look up at Mimi and moan. "I didn't think it'd be on the front page."

She ruffles my curls. "It's wonderful. Just read."

I turn back to the paper.

> Want to know what kind of summer Madison Mitchell is having? Consider that she's batting .425 at cleanup for her league team, Hinton's Grocery, has struck out 15 batters over three games and not made one error and you have to say, what a great summer it is!
>
> "Madison is maybe the most natural athlete I've ever coached," says John Weeks, her coach. "We

count on her a great deal. Plus, she's a pleasure to have around."

Mimi sets the egg pop in front of me and then one at her place. I read about where we live, what grade I'm in, how David taught me to play, how good my dad was as a short-stop at Wisconsin. I read about my mom the lawyer and how I was born in Germany. I hold my breath as my eyes scan the page.

Baseball, however, is not Madison's first love. She likes swimming in the lake, and volleyball is her fa-vorite sport. The talented 12-year-old was a starter for her undefeated sixth-grade volleyball team last year. Jan Post, her coach, says, "Madison is an excep-tional player. We expect great things from her!"

Despite her success on the ball field, she says she won't play middle league next year. She resists any notion that she's a trendsetter, despite knowing that she's the first girl in southern Michigan to play league baseball. Years from now girls will look back at her accomplishments. When asked how she feels about this, she says, "I don't know."

At age 12, when you have everything, it must be easy to wish for more for yourself. But the modest superstar says that if she had one wish in this world, she would wish for the hostages in Iran to be rescued.

A superstar with a social conscience.

You can't ask for much more for the future of our country!

"Ah!" I push the paper away. "Future of our country? Superstar with a social conscience? I sound like such a jerk."

"I think you sound wonderful," Mimi says.

I sit.

"Know what I'm thinking?" she asks. "You're rewriting the rules. And someday this won't be a big deal, girls playing ball with boys. Girls will have their own baseball league. There'll be more options. Not just volleyball, basketball and cheerleading."

I bite into my egg pop. It's cold, but it still tastes good.

"Yeah, but that's not why I'm playing."

"Didn't say it was. But I think that's the way these things happen. People do things because they want to, because they're good. Because, well, because they just should. Then all this happens." Mimi waves her hand over the newspaper.

I look at my picture. My curls aren't sticking out too much. My nose looks small. No way do I look like a boy. Maybe Sara will read this and think about how much she misses me. Maybe she'll call.

"Anyway, it's a lovely article and picture," Mimi says.

"Did Mom see it?"

"Yes, she thought it was lovely, too."

Something about the way she says this makes me lift my eyes and look at her. Did Mom tell her about last night? Mimi has never gotten between us before. But if she asks about my friends, about anything, I'll know for sure.

She opens the paper and eats her egg pop as she reads.

"I've never had my picture in the paper before," I say.

"Nor have I," Mimi says, not looking up. "It's quite something."

I smile, staring at the picture.

"Your mom had her picture in the paper. In high school she won a state debate tournament. In front of two hundred people! The trophy was as big as she was."

I've seen that trophy in Mimi's attic. Mom told me she won the debate arguing that before women got the right to vote, some earlier constitutional amendment should have guaranteed it. I can't remember which amendment. The whole thing was way over my head.

I glance at Mimi. I bet she argued with Mom like crazy when Mom was young. The great big champion debater. "Did you and Mom fight a lot?"

Mimi puts down her fork. "Oh, my, yes."

"About what?"

Mimi looks at me a long time before answering. "Oh, the usual things. In junior high school she had some friends I didn't particularly like. When she got older, she wanted to stay out later than I thought she should. Things like that."

"Didn't it bug you that she dressed like such a hippie?" I've seen the pictures. Mom's hair was wilder and blonder and she wore big round glasses tinted purple.

Mimi smiles. "Some. But I didn't want to fight over clothes."

I drop my eyes. I shouldn't be so worried about clothes, either.

"I guess I've always believed that what's inside counts most," she says. "Not how you look. And I always loved and respected that inner part of your mom."

I roll my eyes. That's so corny, even if it comes from Mimi. But still my cheeks redden. That inner part. I know about this. It's that thing inside that makes you ask questions about yourself. That knows the truth. But it's hard to listen to that voice, especially when other stuff gets in the way.

I look at my picture again. I'm an important member of my team. This year we could win the championships, and part of the reason is me.

16

That afternoon I stand on Crystal's stoop and look through the screen. When I ring the bell, Huey comes to the door dressed in David's shorts and shirt. Through the screen he looks young, as if he just came from gym class.

"Well, did you see it?" I hold my copy of the newspaper behind my back.

Huey rubs his eyes and opens the door. When he squints, his face breaks into a million wrinkles. "See what?"

I thrust the newspaper into his face. He takes it, steps out on the stoop and sits. As he reads, I glance at his left hand. No wedding ring. He finishes and looks up at me.

"You sounded good. Even about the hostages." He grins.

"He asked me what I wished for and I didn't want to be too revealing."

He grins again, then yawns. I sit next to him. Is he really married?

"So, I guess that's all over with, huh?" I say.

"Well, not really. It's on the front page and everyone will see it. You'll have to smile and thank people who comment on it. Because everyone will talk about it."

I haven't seen Huey since the night he argued with Crystal. I bet he has a wife. Kids. And he can't stand to be away from them. "So do you still have writer's block?"

Huey chuckles and rubs his chin. "Yeah, well, I guess you can say that."

"My brother says you're married."

He sits up. "Yeah . . . got married five years ago. But we don't live together. We're taking a break."

"So, this is your break? With Crystal?"

"Oh I see where you're going with this." He nods. "Crystal knows I'm married. She knew from the very first day we met."

"Do you have any kids? Are you going to get a divorce now?"

Huey turns to me and twists his lips to the side. "You sure ask a lot of questions."

I look at the sand. Next to Huey there's a stack of cigarette butts several inches tall. I don't know why I want to know. But it seems as if I'll burst unless I get the answer.

"I don't know about a divorce yet." Huey sighs and lights a cigarette. "And no kids, which is probably good. I don't think I'd make a very good parent."

He's not too healthy, with all the smoking and sleeping he does. And he's never home. Still, he's the easiest person in the world to talk to. I think he'd make a great dad.

"Let me tell you, love is something." He shakes his head and blows a smoke ring over my head.

I'm pretty sure I've never been in love. Mostly what I feel with Tommy is nervous. "I wouldn't know."

"You will someday. And let me tell you, it's complicated." Huey stubs out his cigarette and adds it to the pile. He points to my picture. "Look at you. What a big deal. First girl in southern Michigan. And you're the star."

He's teasing. I straighten. "I'm just playing this year. I'll probably do something else next year, not sports, though." Why'd I say that? I love sports.

Huey smiles. "Why? Are you worried what people will think?"

I shrug. How can I explain something I can't even figure out myself?

"You're a feisty kid, you know that? You should do what you like. Enjoy what you're good at. Do it now, before you're too old like me and it's too late."

Too late? I think of all his hits. "Hopeless, Helpless," "Wasted Nights," "Can't Catch Me."

"You're not old." But even as I say this, I'm not sure. "You wrote great songs."

Huey shakes his hair behind him. "Nice try. But I'm afraid the world is through with a washed-up thirty-nine-year-old rock star."

That night I meet Brett at bus stop 20 and we ride to the baseball field on the other side of Long Beach to watch Billy's team play. When we see the field ahead, I think we have the wrong day. No cars line the street and the side fences are empty. "Are you sure it's not just practice?"

"Yep."

We ride closer, and I see Billy on the mound, his team spread out around him. Groups of parents sit in lawn chairs behind each bench. We stop along the first-base line, behind Billy's bench. Mr. Evans leans on the fence near us, his cap dipped low over his forehead.

"Where is everyone?" I count just twenty people.

"More people come to our games because of you."

It's true, but I'm really glad he's not making a big deal out of it.

Billy winds up and throws. His motion is quick and his arm comes out to the side, not over his head. Still, the ball roars over the plate and into the catcher's mitt for a ball. "He's fast like Randy."

"Yeah, but look how jerky his motion is. He also doesn't have a curveball. You're more consistent than both of them put together."

Billy throws three more pitches, all balls. The batter trots to first base.

"Get your head in the game, Billy," Mr. Evans yells.

Billy nods. I feel a pinch in my chest. How great would it be to stand on the mound and know your dad was right there, watching everything you did?

In the second and third innings Billy strikes everyone out. In the fourth, he throws eight straight balls and walks two batters. The next batter hits a double, and now the game is tied, two to two.

"What are you doing?" Mr. Evans yells. He starts pacing behind the bench.

Billy drops his head and kicks the rubber. His dad should stand still and not yell.

When Billy walks the next batter, Mr. Evans grunts and folds his arms. He's behind the backstop now so we only hear parts of his mumbles. "*No discipline.*" "*Lazy pitches.*" Then, "*You pitch like a girl.*"

"Did he say what I think he said?" Brett asks. I nod. "Well, that's a compliment, seeing you're the only girl pitching these days."

I don't laugh. Several parents turn and glance at me. I look right back.

Billy stands on the mound, his head down. He's not having a very good game, that's for sure. Serves him right. But another part of me begins to feel something else. Maybe even sorry for him.

In the last inning Billy's team scores four runs and wins the game. Brett and I ride home. Sweat drips down my back and dots my upper lip. Billy has speed but he's even wilder than Randy. His motion isn't as good. And there's another difference between them, only I can't figure it out.

"Billy's fast," I say.

"Yeah, but he's all over the place. You, me and Tommy can hit him. Doug, too, if he ever gets out of his slump."

As we turn onto Lake Shore I keep thinking about Billy. And how his dad treated him.

* * *

The next day I go to the pharmacy and buy a tube of Wild Cherry lip gloss. I roll it across the back of my hand, bring my hand to my face and look in the mirror.

Does Crystal wear lip gloss? Can Huey taste it? I pucker my lips. I imagine Tommy's arms around me, my head thrown back, his mouth against mine. I'll wear this lip gloss around the house. When school starts I'll know how to stand at the mirror with the other girls and put it on. I put the tube in the bag.

"Look who's here!"

I whirl around. Sara's mom starts up the aisle. She wears a white tennis dress with yellow trim and white socks with yellow fluffy balls attached to the back. Her gold earrings match her bracelet, and her lipstick is as red as a tomato. She looks as if she just stepped out of a magazine.

Sara trails behind her. She also wears a tennis dress, although it's too small and she keeps pulling at the hem. The hair along her temples and forehead is wet with sweat. Her shoulders hunch forward and she looks at everything in the store except me.

"I was just talking about you," Mrs. Cavanaugh says. "I saw the article in the paper. *Everyone* did. My goodness! I said to Dean, we have to get out and see you play."

It's pretty obvious from Mrs. Cavanaugh's excitement that she doesn't know Sara and I haven't spoken in weeks. I glance at Sara's hands but she keeps them in fists at her sides. Is she wearing her mood ring?

"I said to Sara, why don't we see Madison anymore? And she said baseball is taking so much of your time."

I smile at Mrs. Cavanaugh. Then the pharmacist calls

her name, and she leaves Sara and me alone. I hold the bag behind my back.

Sara shifts her feet and stares at the toothpaste. I throw my shoulders back and lift my chin.

"I thought you hated tennis," I say. That's what she told me last year.

"My mom thinks it would be a good sport for me to play."

We don't say anything for a moment.

"So where's Casey?" I ask.

Sara glances at me, her eyes soft.

I hesitate but can't stop now. "Does she allow you out of the house without her?"

Sara frowns. "What's that supposed to mean?"

"Doesn't she tell you what to do and who you're supposed to be friends with?"

"She doesn't tell me what to do. She's just fun."

"Oh, making fun of people is fun?"

"You should talk." Sara turns from me.

I suck in my cheeks. Behind my back I flip the bag from one sweaty hand to the other. "What do you mean?"

"You haven't been exactly nice, either."

"Like when?"

"Like all the time! Like that day after spring break when you said our hair looked like we'd used a whole can of hairspray on it. You said that in front of *everyone*."

I'd forgotten that. We were in the locker room after gym class. Sara played only a couple of minutes of basketball before sitting on the sideline with Casey. That had been Casey's first week at our school.

"You were so mean," Sara says.

"Well, you left me that day in the cafeteria. You laughed at me because of the fight and then you *left* me there."

"You took off your ring and threw it! I wasn't going to leave until you did that!"

I can't look at her because now I'm totally confused.

We both turn as Mrs. Cavanaugh comes down the aisle. Her smile fades.

"Why such long faces? I've got an idea. We're headed to the pool. Why don't you come along, Madison? We'll stay and have dinner on the deck."

Club sandwiches with pickle slices and endless pop refills. Playing Marco Polo in the pool and then catching fireflies in the plastic cups the bartender gives us. We've done this together every summer since second grade.

But Sara scowls at the floor.

"Thanks, but I've got to get home."

"I don't know what's going on with you girls," Mrs. Cavanaugh says.

"Bye, Mrs. Cavanaugh," I say. "Bye, Sara."

"Bye," Sara says, just above a whisper.

As I ride home I remember what Mimi said. It's what's inside that counts.

No. Friends are the most important thing. And I don't have my best friend anymore.

17

The next game is against Long Beach Realty. When I head through the church parking lot toward the field, I slam on my brakes. The game is still twenty minutes from starting, but the stands are filled. People line the fences in the outfield and along both sidelines. I start counting, then give up. There must be a hundred and fifty people here.

"Hey, Madison!" someone yells as I ride past.

"Hey, superstar!" someone else yells.

"I saw your picture in the paper!" a woman says.

I smile and nod. Brett meets me at the bike rack.

"So many people are here," I say.

"Probably more than at the July Fourth fireworks."

My mouth drops open, and I look over his shoulder at the crowd.

"Just kidding. Come on, let's go warm up."

We walk toward our bench. People pat me on the back. Kids stare. A friend of Mom's hugs me. "What a great article!"

What am I supposed to say? I look for Mom in the bleachers, but I can't find her.

Brett and I start throwing along the first-base line. Mrs. Tulliver and Mrs. Frazier are in lawn chairs behind us, their kids playing in the grass near them. Mrs. Post talks with Mr. Weeks behind the bench. Mimi sits in the top row of the bleachers.

Near the maple tree Artie and D.J. sell lemonade and Coke out of a cooler under a card table. "Hey, Madness!" D.J. yells. "After the game you can sell autographs, and we'll split the profits!"

I try to smile. Then I rub the ball between my fingers and thumb and close my eyes. The leather is tough and soft at the same time. I open my eyes and fire into Brett's mitt.

David leans on the fence, his baseball cap pulled low over his eyebrows. "You're bending your elbow too much to the side again. Come up and over."

I pitch several times. Now I notice it. I rear back, re-membering how Randy kept his arm straight. When I feel my elbow bending to the side, I stop. I start again, and this time I extend my arm upward, putting my body into the ball as I come around.

David nods and I say, "Thanks."

"You must be Madison." A man wearing a Cubs baseball cap and holding a notebook comes up next to David. "I'm Rusty Watts, from the Associated Press."

153

Brett stands up and walks toward me. I smooth out my curls. Do I look as sweaty as he does? I tug at my bathing suit, which is glued to my sides.

"That article about you was put out on the wire, and I thought I'd come down from Chicago and check out your games for myself. Think we could talk after?"

"Well, I don't really have much else to say."

He looks around and then smiles. "I guess this is pretty intimidating."

"It's just baseball. Besides, there must be girls in Chicago who've done this."

"Well, sure, but you're the star."

"But what about everyone else? Our team is really good." Brian hasn't made an error all season, either, and Brett always gets on base. Tommy is a solid hitter. And Doug is in a slump but he's only eleven and he's got a great swing.

"You're the girl," Rusty Watts says.

I glance at Randy. He's on third, fielding grounders. If I weren't here, he'd be the star. But not enough of a star for a story to be written about him. The only reason this is such a big deal is because I'm a girl.

"It's time!" Mr. Weeks calls.

"I have to go," I say, and run to Mr. Weeks.

"The pitcher is fast but a little wild." Mr. Weeks's voice is louder than usual. I step in closer, trying to hear him over the noise from the crowd.

"There are ninety-two people in the bleachers," Donny says. Everyone looks. My throat is dry. I wish our games were like practices.

"Let's just stay focused on what we're doing," Mr. Weeks says. Everyone breaks from the circle. "Hold on, Madison."

Brett puts on a batting helmet and the others sit on the bench.

"This is a lot to handle," Mr. Weeks says, his brown eyes staring into mine. "Are you okay?"

I nod. "Thanks."

Brett stands at the plate and spits into his hands and rubs them on his bat. Donny squeezes between me and Brian. We watch Brett take the first pitch. Ball one.

"There's Billy Evans." Donny squints up at me. Behind the other bench, Billy sits on a ten-speed, his arms crossed.

"Are you scared he's going to try and bean you?" Brian asks.

"Are you kidding? His ball will just bounce right off me. Then I'll bean him back." I smile and Donny giggles. But I can't swallow that lump in my throat.

Brett singles and I move to the end of the bench and put on a batting helmet. Doug strikes out and Tommy hits a single. I step to the plate, men on third and first with only one out. It's muggy and cloudy, and I tug at my suit and glance down at my chest. At least my breasts are staying in place.

"She's no batter," the shortstop says.

I dig my toe into the dirt and watch the first pitch. Strike.

"Don't let her get a hit off you!" a man yells from the crowd.

I swing at the next pitch. Strike!

Concentrate. Did my dad ever have moments like this when he played? Probably not. You don't get to be a Big Ten baseball player by getting rattled.

"Strike the girl out!"

I smack the plate with my bat. The next pitch seems to float toward me. I swing and hit it into right field. I watch it bounce between the outfielders as I round second and stop on third. A triple.

Hinton's two, Long Beach Realty zero.

The boys jump off our bench and cheer. Brett pumps his fist. Even Randy gets off the bench and stands at the fence. When he sees me looking at him, he nods.

On the mound I don't get rattled. I walk two batters but throw lots of strikes and give up only a few hits. But the other pitcher is really good; I strike out twice. It's a tight game. By the last inning, thanks to a double play by Doug, the other team hasn't scored. It's still two to zero. I kick the rubber, then stare into Brett's mitt. I throw and the batter pops up to Tommy. Game over.

My teammates flood the mound. Donny grabs me around my waist and hugs me. Brett slaps my shoulder. Mom and David rush up, clapping. "Attagirl, Madison!" someone yells from the bleachers.

Now the crowd doesn't look so big, and I don't care what anyone yells at me. The game is over and we won.

We have a quick meeting on the bench.

"Nice game, everyone," Mr. Weeks says. "Our team and Johnson Electric are still the only undefeated teams in the league. Everyone else has at least two losses. If both of us win our next games, we'll play a final one to decide the championship."

"What if one of us loses?" I ask.

"Then the other team will automatically be champion. If we both lose, we'll play a deciding game."

"We can do it," Brett says. The others nod.

"We'll have a tough game," Mr. Weeks says. "Long Beach Savings has some good hitters, so let's all be ready."

As Brett and I put away the equipment, I look for Tommy, but he's disappeared in the crowd. Randy goes back out onto the field. I watch as he winds up and throws to Mr. Weeks. He's got to be just as hot and tired as we are.

Sweat drips down my face. I pitched well tonight, but now I just want to go home.

Rusty Watts talks with Mr. Weeks while he catches Randy. I'd forgotten about him. At the bike rack, Tommy is unlocking his bike. Casey, Gina and Sara watch. How fast can I get out of here?

"Wow, Madison, that was a great picture in the newspaper," Casey says.

"Thanks."

Casey wears a choker necklace and hoop earrings and her shirt is tight across her chest. She's lucky—her breasts aren't so big that she has to hide them.

"*You* read the newspaper?" Brett asks.

Tommy bursts out laughing.

I wrap my lock around my seat and pull my bike out of the rack. Sara stares at the ground, her hands in her pockets.

Casey turns to Tommy. "So are you coming with us?"

She stares at him and I realize: Casey *likes* him.

Tommy looks at me. "Want to go into town with us?" He turns to Casey. "Madison can come, right?"

157

Casey smiles. "Sure. The more the merrier."

"Why do you want to go to town?" Brett asks me.

Tingles run up the inside of my legs. Tommy wants me along. He likes me! I want to freeze this moment, make it last. I smile at Tommy, then at Casey.

"Okay, get your bikes," Tommy says.

"We don't have bikes," Casey says.

"You can ride on the back of mine," Tommy says. "Hold on to me."

Casey smiles. Are Gina and Sara supposed to ride on the back of Brett's and my bikes? Or will Casey leave them here? Now I don't know *who* Tommy likes.

And what will we do in town? I don't want to be stuck at the Dairy Queen in my sweaty uniform or dragged through the pharmacy as Casey goes down the aisles fingering lip gloss and nail polish.

Rusty Watts approaches.

"I'm going home," I say.

"Good, let's go," Brett says. We start for the street.

"Wait," Tommy calls. "I'm coming with you!"

He catches up with us and we ride fast, running stop signs and speeding around corners. First Brett's in the lead, then Tommy, then me. My lungs and legs burn and inside I'm shouting: Tommy left Casey! He's coming with me.

We turn onto Lake Shore Drive and ride side by side, pushing each other. When we turn down the hill, Brett pulls ahead. He skids into my driveway, drops his bike and races to the porch.

His baseball shirt hangs down his thighs. Sweat drips off

the end of his pointy nose, and dirt smudges his forehead and cheeks. "I win! I beat you!"

Tommy brings down his kickstand. He sits on the porch. "I didn't know we were racing."

"Yeah, right." Brett sucks in air.

Sweat trickles down my face. I wipe it away with the back of my hand when neither of them is looking. I want to swim, but Tommy doesn't like the lake. What does he like to do, anyway?

"One more game and we could be the champs." Brett stands in front of us.

"How good is Long Beach Savings?" I ask.

"Really good," Tommy says. "Cal Wood hits cleanup. Gary Mason is a good hitter, too."

"Gary hits like he's got a nail in his butt." Brett pretends to hold a bat, squats and sticks his rear out behind him. Tommy and I laugh.

"This is how Cal bats." Brett straightens, his arms holding an imaginary bat above his head. Then he takes a giant step and swings and falls. We can't stop laughing.

Tommy calls out names of people for Brett to imitate and we keep laughing. My legs are jittery. Tommy's next to me. And Brett is so funny.

"How about some lemonade?" Mom stands at the screen.

I follow her inside.

David and Artie sit at the table in their bathing suits.

"You've got your hands full." David whistles.

I ignore him and fill three glasses. David makes a kissing noise. Artie bursts out laughing.

"Shut up, David. I don't tease you about being in love with Tina Phillips."

David's cheeks redden. Artie snickers.

"Madison," Mom says, low. "Be careful."

"I'm not going to spill."

"That's not what I meant. Be careful of his feelings."

"What?" I hurry through the living room. She means be careful of Brett's feelings. But I'm not doing anything wrong. It's not my fault Brett and Tommy came here at the same time.

Tommy jumps up and holds the door open. I hand out the drinks and sit, and Tommy scoots so close that our knees touch. I practically stop breathing. Brett stands in front of us, staring at our knees. Then Tommy reaches for my hand and holds it in his lap.

Brett stops talking and looks out at the street. We all do.

It's dark and the temperature hasn't changed, but chills race up my back. Tommy squeezes my hand, but I'm too nervous to squeeze back. My hand feels numb, as if it doesn't belong to me anymore. I giggle.

"Well, I have to go," Brett says.

He puts his glass on the porch, picks up his bike and says, "Bye," over his shoulder. As I watch him disappear into the dark, I feel my heart sink back into my chest. I've hurt his feelings.

"He's so funny," Tommy says. "I wish I could do that."

Be careful. Brett likes me. I like hanging out with him, he's fun and easy to talk to. But I can't imagine holding his hand.

I sneak a look at Tommy. The sun has bleached his eyebrows white, and I love how the end of his nose turns up slightly. He left Casey. Think of something to say. "Are you friends with Brett?"

"Sure."

I nod. But I doubt Brett would call Tommy a friend.

Tommy begins tickling the top of my hand with the fingers of his other hand. A million tingles race through my body.

"It's so hot," I say.

"Yeah."

"It's supposed to stay hot like this for another week."

"Who says?"

"The newspaper."

"Oh."

He squeezes my hand and when I look at him he leans over and kisses me on the lips. I sit straight, my eyes wide, my breath stuck halfway up my throat. His lips feel soft and warm. *Oh, baby, baby.* Did Crystal feel these little tingles when Huey kissed her? But wait. I pull my hand away. "Don't you have a girlfriend?"

"Yeah. She's up in Boyne for the summer with her grandma."

"Why are you here if she's your girlfriend?" I start to rub where my mood ring used to be.

"I don't know. I like you."

I'm so nervous that all I can say is "Why?"

"What? Why do I like you?"

I nod.

Tommy's blue eyes widen. "Because. I don't know. You're a good pitcher and everything. And you're famous. Everyone knows you."

He likes me because I'm a *good pitcher*? Because I'm

famous? "If no one knew me, then you wouldn't like me?"

"Huh?"

"What?"

"I don't know! I've never had a girl ask me this before. I mean you're pretty, too, I guess."

We stare into the dark. I jump when someone turns on a light in the living room and light floods onto the porch.

We sit there not talking, not looking at each other. When he gets up to go, he kisses me, quickly, then takes off on his bike.

Later I lie in bed with the fan blowing hot air across me. It's easy to remember how it felt when Tommy tickled my hand. It's a lot harder to think about how he doesn't know why he likes me.

But why do I like him?

Who cares? I settle into the pillow. I only want to remember the good things about tonight.

18

The next day Mrs. Frazier stops me to say how much she liked the newspaper article. Mr. Hyde, our mailman, hands me an extra copy for "your scrapbook." Mrs. Post calls to say she's proud of me. "I thought you sounded very mature and confident."

"Thanks." That was Huey's coaching. Even the hostage comment. I hang up and twist the phone cord in my hand. Only three more days until the last game. Then this all might be over.

On Wednesday the *Chicago Tribune* runs a small article about our team, written by Rusty Watts, the AP reporter. He says my playing style is "natural and aggressive" and that I've taken our small town "by storm."

A girl playing on a boys' team certainly isn't a new phenomenon in some Midwestern communities. But in this small beach community, Madison Mitchell isn't just playing baseball. She's dominating. And this has raised a few eyebrows. "She has an unfair advantage because the boys are afraid of being blamed if she gets hurt," says one parent. "She's so confident, she just psychs everyone out."

Confident? Then why am I so nervous all the time? I take David's glove and a ball and throw against the garage door. I count the balls that land in the square and my heartbeat slows.

That afternoon a TV reporter from Chicago calls and Mimi hands me the phone. I shake my head and run out the back door to bury my feet in the sand.

After a while, Mimi says through the screen, "Let's go to the beach."

The air is thick and still. We sit in the sand, the water around our ankles, and I try to make out the hazy horizon, but the water and sky mix together so I can't tell where one stops and the other starts. The beach stretches for miles in both directions. People are everywhere.

"Lordy, this is the place to be." Mimi wiggles her toes. Her dress is bunched up around her knees, and her legs and ankles are freckly and wrinkly. "This might be the hottest summer we've ever had. And no rain."

I nod. The lake water is warmer than I ever remember for July. People's lawns are burning, even Mrs. Minor's.

"It's going to be a hot game tomorrow night." She nudges me in the shoulder.

"I hope we don't have to play a game after this one," I mutter.

What if we have to play Billy's team after all? If the TV people come back for it and Billy beans me, the whole world will know.

"Why?"

"I guess I don't really like baseball that much."

"Is it that you don't like baseball or you don't like all the attention?"

"I wish I could play and nobody would come to our games or talk about it."

Mimi frowns. "It's gotten a bit out of control, hasn't it?"

I nod.

"Well, you're very brave. Much braver than I could ever be."

I smile and look out over the water. The lake is healthier than it was when we first arrived from Germany. I remember trying not to step on the thousands of dead fish that washed onshore and turning back and seeing Mom just standing there, sobbing.

"Do you remember all those dead fish?"

"Yes, the alewives. Just terrible. Thank goodness it's much cleaner now."

That day when Mom and I walked down the beach, I started crying, too. Most of the dead fish were clustered in groups on the sand, as if they were in families.

"Was the lake always so polluted?" I ask. By this time every summer Sara and I have usually water-skied a half dozen times behind Dr. Cavanaugh's boat.

"Oh, goodness, no."

"Did you come down here when you were a kid?"

Mimi nods. "My favorite memories are of when Gramps and I were first married. We'd sit here and roast hot dogs over a fire and talk about our week. Oh, did we talk. And if it was dark and late, and if no one was here, we'd skinny-dip. Lordy, there's nothing like swimming in the nude."

"Mimi!"

"What? We would! You're old enough to hear this."

I don't want to think about my grandparents naked. Still, we giggle. It's so nice to know they loved each other.

Mimi sits watching while I swim. Then we climb the stairs, cross Lake Shore Drive and turn down my street. The pavement burns my feet, but I'm cool from the water. I run my fingers over my lips. It's been three days since Tommy kissed me. Since then I haven't seen or talked to him.

Maybe he changed his mind about me because I'm a bad kisser. *Am* I a bad kisser? I wish I could talk to Sara about this.

I called Brett two nights ago, but he said he had to mow lawns and couldn't come over.

On our driveway I rinse off my feet with the hose while Mimi goes into the house.

"Hey, neighbor, come here," Huey calls from Crystal's front stoop. His hair is pulled behind him in a ponytail and he wears a new pair of shorts and shirt. I walk down the sidewalk toward him. "Is it always this hot here in the summer?"

"Nah. It's got to rain soon. Where'd you get the clothes?"

166

"Crystal was tired of seeing the striped shirt." Huey sits and shades his eyes as he looks up. "How's the celebrity business?"

"People keep talking about the article. A TV reporter wants to come to the game tomorrow night and interview me."

He whistles. "Because you're the star. But don't sweat over the TV reporter."

"Why?"

"Remember, dramatic pauses. Don't reveal too much. Print reporters have more space than TV people. TV—they shoot an hour of film and use only a minute. Ask a question if you can't think what to say. Reporters love to talk about themselves."

"Really?"

Huey nods. "Oh, yeah. Most TV people are in the business because they really want to be on the other side of the camera."

I sit next to him. He digs his toe into the sand. His legs are long and thin and hairy and white. Grown-up's legs.

"Would you come to my game?" It might be easier facing the TV people knowing he's there. Or maybe I just want to show him what I can do.

"Oh, I don't know. I haven't been to a baseball game in years."

"That's okay. You don't have to come." I look away so he can't see that I really want him there.

"I'll think about it. Okay?" He smiles and I smile back. "Those boys must hate playing against you. Must be hard for them, worrying about getting struck out by you."

"No." But I remember how happy Tommy was after he smacked that cream puff.

"Their little manhoods are on the line. And I bet they're all crazy about you."

"No way." Randy sure isn't.

"They just don't know it yet. You're tenacious and funny and curious. You like the same things they do. Plus, you have great hair."

"I wish it were straight and thin so I could part it and then it would feather to the side."

"We always want what we don't have, neighbor. You should be glad you're different. Someday you'll love your hair."

"If we win our next game and Billy Evans wins his game, then we have to play a championship game against him," I say. "Billy said he's going to bean me."

Huey lights a cigarette. He raises his hand to throw the match into the grass but then drops it into the pile of butts at his feet. He chuckles. "I bet that kid is sweating in his shorts."

"Not Billy."

"Ah, he's afraid. So he's trying to intimidate you. If you're scared, he has a better chance of making you nervous. Stay calm. Don't let him see your nerves."

"But he's the fastest pitcher in the league."

"Lighten up, neighbor. You'll do great. You're what, twelve? You're just figuring stuff out. Who you are. Crap like that. Take your time. Put yourself in other people's shoes. Think. Everyone has hangups. Everyone gets nervous. You're not alone."

I've never heard him talk like this, so adult-like. Usually he sounds as if he's just woken up. I imagine Billy on the mound, scared that I might get a hit off him. Or Casey in front of her mirror, worrying about how she looks.

I could sit here talking to Huey all day.

"Course, then you grow up and have other problems."

Like writer's block? Maybe he misses his wife, even if they are taking a break. Maybe Crystal's still mad at him.

I want to help him, the way he's helped me. No one else seems to understand what has happened to me this summer.

"When I was writing my English essay, I couldn't think of anything to say so I kept writing in my notebook until something came to me." I peek at Huey. "I could go down to the pharmacy and get you a notebook."

"Think that might help my writer's block?" he asks. I nod. "Okay."

"And with Crystal, I think you should know . . . Well."

Huey watches me and waits. He should know that Crystal isn't who he thinks she is. If Crystal hasn't told him about her mom dying, she probably hasn't told him about the snowstorm, either.

"Crystal is kind of "—I lower my voice—"a maniac."

"A what?"

"A couple of years ago we had this big snowstorm. It was the night Crystal's mom had a heart attack, I think. Crystal was running around in the snow in just her nightgown, her *summer* nightgown. With no slippers or boots or anything. Just running around the streetlight. Back and forth."

Huey's smile fades. He stares out toward the streetlight. "Why did she do that?"

"I don't know."

"Then what happened?"

"My mom went out to help her and my brother made me go upstairs. Then the ambulance came. I already told you the rest."

Huey nods. "Wow, that's sad."

Of course it's sad. But Huey doesn't seem all that worried. *Put yourself in other people's shoes,* he said. Have I missed something?

"Did you drink all the milk?" Crystal stands behind the screen door.

I practically jump off the stoop. I thought she was out!

Crystal wears cutoffs and a tight red T-shirt. When her necklace catches the sun it sends a streak of light back out through the screen.

"Oh, yeah." Huey stands and opens the door. Crystal glares down at me. Did she hear what I said?

They disappear into the house and I start down the walk. I stop and look up at the streetlight. The night of the storm, the snow fell sideways in the wind as it coated the pole. Around and around Crystal went, her arms out in front of her as if she were blind and had to feel her way.

I put both hands on the pole. The metal is cool and smooth. What happened to make Crystal do this? What did she see?

How would I act if my mom had a heart attack in front of me? I squeeze the pole, then run home as fast as I can. Mimi is on the phone in the kitchen. I rush in and throw my arms around her waist. She smells like vanilla and basil and I close my eyes and breathe deeply.

"Oh, speak of the devil, here she is." Mimi holds the phone to my ear.

I try to slow my breathing. Is this Brett? Tommy? I glance at the clock. I have to be at the field in ten minutes, but I don't want to let go of Mimi.

"Hello."

"Hi, Madison."

Sara.

19

"What are you doing?" Sara asks.

I let go of Mimi and sit on the floor. "I have practice."

"Oh. I called, you know, to say hi."

"That's good." Should I say I'm sorry?

"Well, maybe you have to go to practice now."

"Yeah."

"I have to go to a *tennis* round robin at the club." She spits the word *tennis*. "I'll talk to you later."

"Okay."

"Okay." She hangs up.

I keep the receiver at my ear. Call her back! I glance at the clock. I run out the door and take off on my bike.

* * *

Most everyone is playing catch in the outfield. I wait for Brett to finish putting on his catching gear. I punch the pocket in my glove, but he doesn't look up.

"Want to warm up?" I can't tell if he's mad at me.

"I should probably catch Randy, since he's pitching tomorrow night." Brett stands.

"Okay. Want to go swimming after practice?"

"I might have to cut more lawns."

He's mad.

"Madison, come catch with us!" Tommy calls from the outfield.

I wave but don't move.

"So, is he your boyfriend now?" Brett asks.

Boyfriend. I have no idea. "Maybe."

"Figures. All the girls go for him."

I nod. See, I'm just like one of the girls.

Still, I feel something sink in my chest as I watch Brett ride away after practice without saying goodbye. I stand next to Tommy at the bike rack.

"Want to go downtown?" he asks. "I'm meeting my brothers at the library. We're skateboarding on the steps. It's really cool. You can watch."

"Watch? Can't I do it with you?" I've never been on a skateboard, but it doesn't look that hard. It's all about balancing, which I'm pretty good at.

"I guess. Usually girls watch. They don't do it."

The tops of my ears sting. I can tell by his smile that he isn't kidding. "Girls can be as good as boys on skateboards."

"I've just never seen any girl do it. But you could try.

173

You'd probably be pretty good, seeing that you're a tomboy and all."

Tommy climbs on his bike. I cross my arms.

"Of course I could do it. I just don't know if I want to."

"Okay, if you change your mind, meet me at the library." He rides away.

I *am* a tomboy. Fine. But . . . does he still like me?

The next night the TV people arrive in the second inning. I'm playing third, my elbows on my knees as I crouch, waiting for Randy's pitch. A man and a woman set up a camera on a tripod just behind the backstop and point the camera at me.

What if I have an itch under my bathing suit? What if I make an error? The whole world will see.

I glance at the runner on second and wait for Randy's pitch. The batter hits a line drive right at me. I catch it and throw to Tommy at second before the runner can get back to the base. A double play. Randy glances at me and nods.

"Attagirl, third basewoman!" A man yells from the stands. Everyone laughs.

I try to find him in the bleachers, but it's too crowded. People are lined up behind the benches and along the baselines. D.J. and Artie are under the maple tree, selling cans of pop. Mrs. Post waves from behind our bench. Did Huey come?

I run to our bench. Concentrate on the game!

When we're up, I walk. Then in the fourth inning I hit

a single that sends Brett home. Randy hits a double and I score. By the last inning we're up, six to five. The game will be over if they don't score and we get two more outs.

I watch Randy wind up and throw. A ball. I glance at the runners on first and second. So far, Randy's walked way too many batters. But at least we're hitting well and no one has made any errors in the infield.

He throws again. The batter hits a soft grounder up the middle. Doug gets it, but his only play is at first. Two outs, but runners advance to third and second. The boy on third stands on the bag, clapping his hands. He pushes the helmet off his forehead. Even standing on the bag, he's a good four inches shorter than me.

Randy winds up and throws. Strike! The crowd cheers. Randy makes a fist with his hand and says "*Yes!*"

"Way to go, Randy!" I yell. It's hard to be mad at someone who has such a perfect pitching motion.

He turns back to the plate. He shakes his long arms out. He pulls up his belt. Mimi would probably say he hasn't come into his body yet. Have I come into mine?

I glance around at the boys. Maybe they're all kind of uncomfortable, too.

Randy throws and the batter hits a grounder down the chalk on the third-base line. Move! The ball isn't that fast! But I hesitate too long and then have to reach across my feet. The ball jumps when it hits a bump and bounces off my glove into left field. I turn, chase it down and throw it home. Too late. Both runs score. The game is over. We lost.

We lost.

The other team swarms over home plate, cheering and screaming. We stay where we are, quiet. Then this sick feeling rumbles through my stomach. I should have gotten into position, but I was afraid. Now I've lost the game. I've lost the game and probably the championship.

What an unbelievable error.

I walk off the field, my head hanging.

"Ah, tough break, Madison," Mr. Weeks says.

I've got to go home because I'm about to cry. But Mr. Weeks tells us to sit on the bench. Randy is at the far end. He'll tell everyone he was right; I shouldn't be playing. Brett will be even madder.

"Okay, you all played a good game." Mr. Weeks stands in front of us. "That was a tough grounder. When it took that bounce it would have been hard for anyone to stop it."

No one says anything. Sure, it was a tough grounder, but I didn't get my body behind my glove. Had I done that, I could have stopped it.

"We don't know what's happening with the other game tonight, so there's still a chance we're in this."

"Small chance," Randy mutters. I cringe.

"Come on, now, chins up," Mr. Weeks says.

I help clean up, avoiding everyone's eyes. No one talks. When it's time to go, I see the TV people coming toward me. I run and find Mom and David.

"Can we go, *please?*" I'm within seconds of bursting into tears.

"Maddie," David starts.

"No, I just want to go home. Now!"

"Come with me," Mom says. "David, will you ride her bike home?"

She doesn't wait for an answer as she turns me toward the parking lot. Once we're in the car and moving, I roll down the window, stick my head out and burst into tears. I can still see that grounder coming at me, then jumping when it hit the bump. I should have gotten my body behind my glove.

"Madison, you played a good game," Mom says. "It's just a bad break that that ball took such a bad bounce and the runs scored."

"I lost the game for my team. The championship! It was my fault!"

"Honey, everyone makes errors."

"But I'm not supposed to make any errors. That newspaper article made me sound like such a star. Now people will say I shouldn't be out there. A girl shouldn't play."

"Who will say that?"

"Everyone!"

She turns onto Lake Shore Drive. Down below, the lake is as still as the air. The tears burn in my eyes. Why can't she understand this?

"You don't know what this is like because you don't play baseball."

"That's true, but I know what it's like to make mistakes."

"No, you don't!"

Mom stops at the stop sign. But instead of turning down the hill toward our house, she looks at me. "Are you serious?"

"Yes!" Certainly she makes little mistakes, like forgetting to go to the grocery store and showing up late all the time. But she always knows what to say. And she never worries about her work, clothes, friends, fitting in.

"I've made plenty." She shakes her head and starts down the hill. "My whole life I've made mistakes."

I turn to her. What mistakes?

Then I feel the hairs on my neck standing straight up. "Like marrying Dad?"

She pauses as she turns into our driveway. "I made plenty with him, but that wasn't one of them. Otherwise I wouldn't have had you or David."

"Then it was a mistake to leave him?" I hold my breath. I want this to be true more than anything I've ever wanted.

"No." She shakes her head, slowly.

"Are you sure? What if he misses us? What if he's dying to know who we are? What if he's really upset and doesn't understand why you took us away?"

She turns off the car but we still sit there. "He knows why we left. He wanted nothing to do with us."

I frown and let out my breath. "You've already told me this."

"But Madison, you've never really heard it. You've never wanted to truly believe it. And I understand that. I know you've always wanted to think of him differently. But you *have* to hear this. Now. The army is the only thing that's important to him."

I feel a sob rising through my chest and into my throat again.

"I didn't make him stay away. I tried everything to reach him. When I told him I wanted to go home, he—Oh, how can I get through to you? I'm sorry. I know this hurts."

"This is *your* fault!"

"How—how is this my fault?" Mom's face is pink.

"If only we'd stayed in Germany. If only he'd gotten to know me!"

But now that I've finally said this out loud, I know it's not true. My dad doesn't want me. He's never wanted me.

I open the car door and run through the yard.

"Madison, wait!"

I climb the sand dune and run past the Phillipses' yard. I take the steps two at a time, cross Lake Shore Drive and stop at the lake. I take off my shoes and uniform and leave everything in the sand. Then I dive into the water and swim to the sandbar.

The water is so cold that soon I'm numb and tingling. I float on my back and look for stars. All these faces swim around in my head—Mom and Dad, Randy, Tommy, Brett, Sara.

I see the first star. Then another. If I can keep finding stars, I won't have to think about anything. By the time I swim to shore I've counted thirty-five. I see David waiting near my clothes. Mom must have told him where to find me.

I glance at him and pick up my uniform and we start walking. Now all I see in my mind is that grounder coming at me.

"Tough break tonight." He takes off his hat and puts it in his back pocket.

"I can't believe I messed everything up." We climb the dune to Lake Shore Drive.

"You didn't move quick enough, that's all. When you're fielding grounders you have to keep your glove between your legs and your body behind your glove."

"I don't think I was meant to play third base," I say. "Not like Dad."

"You think Dad was perfect?"

I shrug. "He didn't make any errors."

"You've got this thing about him," David says. "But remember when I told you he could palm a basketball? I didn't tell you the whole story. That day I was in the yard, playing catch with a kid. Dad came out, reading something. I kept looking at him, hoping he'd watch me. I took my eye off the baseball and it hit me and gave me a bloody lip.

"I cried because it hurt so much. But he never even looked at me. He walked over to the yard, palmed a basketball and stood there holding it, reading. Never asked if I was okay. Never even took his eyes off what he was reading. Finally Mom came out with some ice and took me inside. He just didn't care enough, Mad."

I glance at David. He's a lot of things. A know-it-all. A teaser. But not a liar.

The only clear memory I have of Dad is of him standing outside a screen door. And when I blinked and looked again, he was gone.

"Maybe he just didn't hear you crying."

He shakes his head as we walk up the steps to the Phillipses' yard. We stop and look over the field.

When we first started playing baseball, the field seemed huge and only D.J. could hit the oak tree on the fly. Years later, when Dr. Phillips built the shed and planted some hedges and the oak tree didn't seem so far away, we had to come up with some ground rules. But that's one of the things I loved about baseball. Back then we just made new rules if things didn't seem fair anymore.

"I hope this heat breaks before your game tomorrow night," David says.

"What game?"

"The championship game. Billy's team lost tonight."

"*Lost?*"

He nods. "Mr. Weeks called. Seven to six."

I hug my uniform to my chest as we start walking again. Will the boys even want me to play? "I don't want to play anymore."

"Because of one error? Who cares! Besides, Randy pitched tonight so you're on tomorrow. Just think, you get to pitch in the championship game."

I rub my shoulder. It feels good, strong, rested. But what will I do about Billy? "I just wish I didn't get so nervous."

"What do you have to be so nervous about?"

"How can you ask that? All those people watching. And the reporters."

He shrugs. "Are you kidding? I think it'd be fun."

"It's sort of fun."

"Sort of? Maddie, you're the best player out there. Do you know how many kids would love to say that? To be the best. It's what everyone wants!"

"Not everyone."

"How come you don't love this?"

"You've . . . you've never done this. You're not a girl playing in the boys' league. And you've . . . never been as good as I am. So you don't know what it feels like to have everyone expecting you to be so good or to not make an error." I hold my breath but I don't want to take it back. He's got to understand me, even if I hurt his feelings.

"Yeah, but . . ."

"You only see what you want to see, David."

He frowns, then sighs. "Okay. What exactly makes you nervous?"

"For one thing, Billy Evans says he's going to bean me."

"Punk. When you're up, crowd the plate. Really hang over it. That will show him you're not afraid, and he'll have a tougher time zeroing in on the strike zone. When he's up, pitch inside. Nothing on the outside. That's where he likes it."

Crowd the plate. Pitch inside. I can do that. I glance at David again. He stares at his feet as he walks. I think about the story he told me about Dad. If I'd been playing catch with the neighbor kid all those years ago, I would have caught that baseball. I'm quicker with my hands than David. But maybe catching that ball wouldn't have made a bit of difference with Dad.

"You should be a coach," I say. "You know everything about the game. You're good at explaining things and you always know what to do."

"Oh, now you're buttering me up after insulting me?" He smiles slightly. I grin back. "Maybe I'll help coach your middle-league team next year."

"Middle league?"

"You'll do great."

In the kitchen, Mom is on the phone. She hands it to me.

It's Brett. "Why'd you take off?"

"I just feel so awful about losing the game. Everyone's mad."

"Nobody is mad. Well, except for Randy. But come on, it's okay. You gotta get ready to pitch tomorrow. We're going to win!"

I stretch the phone cord to the screen door and look out. The sky is dark, with thousands of stars. But Mimi said a storm's coming tomorrow. I hope it holds off until after the game. I want to get this over with.

20

I stand at the mirror. Even though I'm wearing my suit, my left breast shoots through the o. Thunder rumbles through my window. The sky is dark gray and still. Not even the birds make a sound.

"Maddie, let's go!" David yells up the stairs.

Mimi, David and I will drive to the game. Mom will come after work. Last night I ate dinner, head down, while Mom tried to talk about our conversation in the car.

"I want to understand why you don't think you're allowed to make errors," she said. "And how you came to believe that I don't make mistakes."

But I was quiet. And this morning I pretended to be asleep when she kissed me goodbye. Maybe if I keep this up, we won't ever have to talk about mistakes or errors or Dad again.

"Finally. Let's go," David says when I walk into the kitchen.

Mimi smiles. "You'll do great."

We drive to the game in silence. I don't look at Crystal's house when we pass by. I'm glad Huey didn't come last night and see that error. But still . . . I wish he'd shown up. I take a deep breath. Today there were three letters to the editor about me. *Let the girl play and leave her alone*, one man wrote. *Madison is our hero*, wrote a woman who said she was the mother of three girls.

In the last letter, someone named Mike Pitts wrote, *Madison Mitchell can hit and pitch, and she's a responsible member of her team. But if she wants to be treated equally, then she also has to take responsibility for any injuries she might get while playing. Just like with a boy, it won't be anyone's fault but her own if she gets hurt.*

Brett's at the curb when Mimi lets me out. The bleachers are nearly full and people are lining up behind the third- and first-base fences.

Brett wears his shin guards and chest protector. He slaps a baseball into my glove. "Come on, let's warm up."

Tommy and Randy are in the infield. I glance at the others and mumble hello. Do they want me here? I can't tell.

We stand off the third-base line. Behind me, Mrs. Jennings and Mrs. Tulliver and their kids sit in lawn chairs. They scream, "Go, Madison!"

I throw easily, pausing after every pitch to look for

Mom. Mimi and David make their way through the bleachers. Someone from the sidelines yells, "Go, girl!" Three young girls behind our bench wave posterboards above their heads. WE LOVE MADISON, the boards say.

Artie and D.J. have set up their refreshment table. Behind the backstop the TV reporters are fixing their camera on top of the tripod. Nothing about me was on the news last night or today. Maybe they're waiting until after this game to air something.

"Where's the girl?" someone yells.

"You okay, Wisconsin?" Brett calls.

I nod. Billy's team forms a huddle on the grass off the first-base line while our team continues to field ground balls on the infield. I watch Tommy scoop up a grounder and throw it to Brian. Even in the gray light, Tommy's hair is bright.

Mr. Weeks stands beside me, watching me pitch.

"Batter up!" The umpire sweeps off the plate.

"Madison," Mr. Weeks says. "Everyone makes mistakes. A champion learns from them. Just pitch your best. We all know what you can do."

"Thanks."

Brett and I walk out onto the field. He pulls down his mask before heading to the plate. "Okay, Wisconsin. No cream puffs. Just throw heat."

I adjust my cap and look to the crowd. David and Mimi are on the top row next to Dr. and Mrs. Cavanaugh. Mimi waves and gives me a thumbs-up.

A short boy comes to the plate, his bat resting on his shoulder. I can tell by his practice swings that he knows what he's doing. I wrap my hand around the ball, wind up and throw. The ball is outside but catches the plate. Strike one.

The crowd cheers. *Go, Madison!* I smooth the front of my shirt and look at the rubber. Concentrate. I throw the next pitch. The boy swings and misses, then slams his bat on the plate. I have him. He swings and misses my next pitch. One out.

The crowd cheers. Someone blows a bullhorn. Mr. Evans stands behind Billy's bench, his arms folded, his legs spread, his cap pulled down to meet the top of his sunglasses. The next batter pops out to Tommy. The third batter steps up. Billy is on deck, stretching with a bat behind his head. He's taller than I remember. And broader through the shoulders. I look at Brett's mitt and throw. The batter hits a slow grounder up the first-base line. I run, grab it with my bare hand and throw it to Brian. Three outs. Before Billy came up!

The crowd erupts as we run off the field. I search the bleachers for my mom. How can she be this late? *Again?*

Brett takes off his equipment and walks to the batter's box. Billy's first pitch screams past; Brett leans back and nearly falls over.

"That's it, show him your stuff!" Mr. Evans yells. Billy nods. Do they talk over every play after games?

Brett taps the plate with his bat and rears back. He swings and sends a line drive at the second baseman. One out. Then Doug walks and Tommy strikes out. I'm up.

"Go, Madison," someone yells.

I adjust my helmet and step into the box. Billy glares at me.

"Hey, batter, batter," the shortstop says.

Billy's pitch comes at me like a bullet. I throw myself backward. The ball zings over my head and into the backstop. Doug runs to second. Ball one.

"Boo," Donny yells from the bench. "Boo!"

"Hang in there, Wisconsin!" Brett yells.

Hang in there? How can I crowd the plate without getting hit?

I step back in the box, lean over the plate and wait. Billy's ball whizzes into the catcher's mitt. But it's outside. Ball two.

"Settle down!" Mr. Evans yells. Billy kicks the rubber and doesn't look up.

I glance back at the bleachers. Mom squeezes through the crowd. I step back into the box, take a deep breath and let the next pitch scream past me. Ball three.

Billy's fast, like Randy, but his motion is rushed. Does he even know where his ball is going?

The next pitch roars toward me and I swing, sending the ball over the third-base umpire's head for a foul ball. What would David tell me? Swing earlier. Don't take such a big backswing. All I need is a hit.

Billy's next pitch is high and outside. Ball four. I jog to first base and stand on the bag. He didn't bean me. I didn't strike out.

Randy walks and I jog to second. The bases are loaded and Donny is up. He stands at the plate, pushing his helmet off his face. Billy motions for the infielders to move in and everyone takes a few steps forward. I point to Donny's feet and he glances down, nodding. He swings at the first pitch, his feet solid, and sends a blooper over first base.

The crowd cheers. I run to third and Doug runs home. Safe! We're up one to nothing. Donny jumps up and down on the first-base bag, yelling, "I got a hit! I got a hit!"

"Way to go!" I yell. Our team is off the bench, cheering. Billy kicks the rubber and scowls at Donny.

He strikes out Brian on three pitches and the crowd moans. I take a big breath and trot in. At least we're ahead.

I jog to the bench to get my glove. Brett meets me on the mound. "We're on the board now. Just throw smoke."

Billy stands in the batter's box. I'll keep the ball inside, just as David told me. I rear back and throw. Ball one. I throw again. Ball two. Billy steps out of the box and practice-swings. When he's ready, I throw again. Ball three.

"She's no pitcher!" someone yells from the sidelines.

Why can't I throw strikes? I close my eyes and see how that grounder bounced off my glove last night. I cringe. No more errors. I take a deep breath and open my eyes. My fingers and palms are cold. My knees shake.

Concentrate!

I throw the next pitch. Billy hits a ground ball up the middle. The crowd cheers as he runs to first base.

"Pitches like a girl!" someone yells.

So what? I am a girl. I glance at Randy but he doesn't look at me.

The next batter stands at the plate. He's short and skinny and keeps pushing the helmet out of his eyes. I clutch the ball along the seams and throw. Strike one. Strike two. Then I strike him out, and the next two batters, too.

Why didn't I pitch like that against Billy? But at least he only got a single off me.

In the second inning Billy walks two batters. Then he strikes out the next three.

His dad yells from behind the bench after nearly every pitch. "Keep your head down! Lift your front leg! Slow down! Think before you throw. *What are you doing now?*"

Billy frowns and turns his back to his dad. I sure wouldn't want my dad yelling like that.

In the third, Billy and I walk each other. In the sixth inning Billy's catcher hits a triple off me and then comes home on a single to right field. The score is one to one.

When we're up, Brian and Brett strike out. Doug walks, then makes it to third when Tommy singles to right field. With two outs, I stand at the plate and wipe my clammy hands on my pants. I'm ready to get a hit! But Billy walks me and now the bases are loaded.

Randy is up next and he hits the first pitch, a grounder to the second baseman. Doug takes off for home. The second baseman scoops up the ball. All he has to do is step on his bag for the last out, but in a panic he throws to the plate. I run to second.

"Slide!" Brett screams to Doug from the bench.

The catcher stands in front of the plate, his body rising to catch the ball. Doug dives headfirst to the left of him, catching the plate with his right arm.

"Safe!" the umpire yells.

The crowd explodes. My teammates run to the fence, congratulating Doug as he jogs to the bench. Brett screams, "We're gonna win. We're gonna win!"

"Nice belly flop!" Randy yells. He grins at me.

I stand on second base and pump my fist. My heart is pounding. I want to win! I jump, turning in midair. I land facing the outfield. And there's Huey, way out along the center field fence, alone. He wears David's green-and-white-striped T-shirt.

I stop myself from waving—I want to be cool—but I'm grinning as I turn back to the field. Here we go!

The crowd quiets. Billy stands with his back to the plate, his head down.

"Get your head in the game," Mr. Evans shouts.

I cringe. *Stop yelling!*

Donny is up. He pulls up his baggy pants, finds a bat and puts it on his shoulder.

"Remember your feet!" I yell.

He nods and walks to the plate. He stands with his feet evenly placed, his bat back. Billy winds up and throws. The ball screams through the air and hits Donny in the chest, knocking him off his feet. He lies in the dirt, not moving. I run to the plate as the umpire calls, "Time out."

Donny is whimpering, trying not to cry. The umpire squats and helps him take off his helmet, then undoes the top couple of buttons on his shirt. A red spot, the exact size of the ball, glows on his chest next to his heart. Big tears start to fall down his dirty cheeks.

"Are you okay?" I'm shaking as I crouch.

"Oh, boy, that looks sore," Mr. Weeks says. "Can you stand?"

"I'm okay, I'm okay," Donny cries.

"Do you think something's broken?" I ask the umpire.

He shakes his head. "Nah, just a nasty bruise. He'll be fine."

Donny wipes the tears with the back of his hand, and we help him up. The crowd applauds as Mr. Weeks walks him off the field. His mom waits with ice wrapped in a towel. He sits on the bench, the ice clutched to his chest, his face streaked with dirt and tears. I whirl around and glare at Billy. He stands, one hand on his hip, as if he's bored with the whole thing.

What a jerk! It's one thing to say he's going to bean me. I'm his age and as big as he is. But Donny? When Billy's at bat, I'm going to hit him. I don't care what happens.

Billy has walked in a run by hitting Donny. It's three to one. I jog to third and Mr. Weeks sends Doug to first base to run for Donny. Brian steps into the box. Billy throws two balls. Mr. Evans yells, "Get your head in the game, Billy!"

I look at Donny, who holds the ice to his chest. But at least he's no longer crying.

Brian strikes out on three pitches, and I run to get my glove. Let's end this game. Brett meets me on the mound. He pushes his mask off his face. "This is it. One, two, three and we win. Then you won't have to pitch to Billy. Don't let up, Wisconsin."

"Okay," I say. He squeezes the ball and puts it in my glove.

I strike out the first batter. The second hits a fly over Randy's head. Randy runs after it, but the runner is fast and makes it to second. The third batter hits a double and the runner scores. Now it's three to two.

The next batter grounds out to Tommy, but the runner makes it to third. Now Billy is up, with a man on third and two outs.

One more out and we'll win. Concentrate.

I glance out at center field. Black clouds have moved over the outfield. Huey is still there. He raises a fist. Then I look up at Mom, who's holding her face in her hands. Everyone in the bleachers is standing, yelling and clapping. Mrs. Frazier and Mrs. Tulliver are hugging and shouting. "You can do it, Madison!" The TV camera is pointing at me.

"Go for it, Madness!" D.J. yells from a branch of the maple tree.

My legs are rubbery. I feel the texture of the seam and the scuff marks on the ball. A minute ago I was so angry that I was going to bean Billy.

But if I hit him, that would put two men on base, and what if I can't strike out the next batter? A big gamble.

I glance around the horn. Randy pounds his fist into his glove. Doug blows a bubble with his gum. Tommy smiles. Brian gives me a thumbs-up.

I turn back to the plate. Billy takes a practice swing; then he's ready.

I hit him in the cafeteria, and it made everything worse.

I throw the first pitch. Ball.

Maybe the safe thing to do is to walk him. Then I'll just have to take my chances against the next batter. I throw another ball. Billy steps out of the box and takes a practice swing.

"Get back in there, Bill," Mr. Evans yells.

He would be so happy if Billy got a hit. But if he grounds out? Strikes out?

I raise my glove and dig the ball into the pocket. Don't think like this. Billy doesn't deserve it. *Donny.*

I throw the ball low and inside, and Billy swings and misses. He watches the next pitch go by. Strike two. The crowd cheers and whistles. Someone blows the bullhorn.

Billy slams his bat on the plate and turns to the umpire. "That ball was way low!"

"Boo!" Donny yells from the bench. "Bad sport!"

I take off my cap and wipe my forehead on my sleeve. Every nerve in my body seems to twitch.

People yell, "Don't let the girl strike you out!"

"Come on, Madison, you can do it!"

"But the ball was low!" Billy says to the umpire.

"You'll walk home by yourself if you don't get back in the box!" Mr. Evans yells.

Brett and the infielders meet me on the mound.

"Look, Madison," Randy begins. I cross my arms. "Look where Billy's standing."

Billy's at the far edge of the batter's box, bat ready.

"Yeah. He's expecting it inside again. So I'm going low and outside."

Randy nods. "You can do it."

"We're with you, Wisconsin." Brett runs back to the plate.

I close my fingers around the seams and take a deep breath. Billy glares at me. I lean back and throw. The ball is outside and a little too high—I feel it when I let go. Billy reaches across the plate and swings anyway. Misses.

He throws his bat into the backstop. Strike three. Game over.

The crowd screams. Brett runs to the mound and picks me up around my waist and twirls me. The rest of the team swarms around us.

"We did it! We won! We won!" Brett yells.

We all did. Fielding. Donny with his first hit. Doug sliding into home.

People flood the field. Mrs. Frazier and Mrs. Tulliver sandwich me in a hug. David pushes through the crowd and slaps me on the back. I glance to the outfield but Huey is gone. Then Randy reaches across the crowd and grabs my sleeve.

"You did a great job, Madison. You really did."

"You too."

"You were terrific." Mom's hands are knitted together in front of her, and she doesn't try to hug me. Then someone pushes her away and I'm thrown up against Sara.

"It's so cool! You struck him out!" Her dark hair is frizzy, especially on top. We look at each other.

"I'm sorry about everything," I say.

"Me too," she says, then fast, "Casey grabbed a note I was writing to you and read it, that's how she knew about the baseball. I didn't mean to tell her. Then you said I was going to leave you in the cafeteria, which I wasn't going to do! Until you threw your ring away and that made me so mad at you. How could you do that?"

We both turn when thunder cracks over the trees. A cool breeze sweeps across the field. "I don't know. I saw you back up that day and thought you just didn't care.

And you were thinking about quitting volleyball. And then Casey . . ."

"Casey kind of makes you do things. It's like you can't help yourself. I guess that's pretty lame." She looks down.

I nod. I remember standing in the bathroom, watching Casey's reflection in the mirror and wanting so much for her to pay attention to me. If you're the person she picks, it must be the greatest feeling. For a while.

"I'm sorry about the ring."

Sara shrugs. "They didn't really work that great, anyway."

Brett grabs me by the arm and pulls me toward the bench.

"Come over tomorrow," I call to Sara. "Let's go swimming."

She grins. "Okay!"

Brett and I pack up the equipment as fast as we can. People hurry from the field. The TV reporters talk with Mr. Weeks, and one keeps looking at me. I turn away. The season is over. We won. And Sara and I are friends again.

"I suppose you're going off with your boyfriend to town or something." Brett doesn't flinch when a huge clap of thunder cracks over us.

"He's not my boyfriend."

Brett raises his eyebrows. "Do you think you'll have another boyfriend soon?"

Be careful with his feelings. "I—I don't know."

The smile drops off his face.

"Come over tomorrow," I say. "The waves are going to be great after this storm."

"Yeah, okay!" He leans in close. "Wisconsin, we won!" He runs off, laughing.

When the rain comes, it makes a sizzling sound as it hits the pavement around the bleachers. Mr. Weeks and the reporters race off the field. I lift my head and let the cool drops sting my face.

Billy and his dad start toward the street. I'm so glad we won. I'm glad I struck him out. Yes! But I was lucky. He should never have swung at that pitch.

Billy walks slowly, as if it isn't pouring, his head down, an equipment bag over his shoulder. Disappointing your dad must feel pretty lousy.

But it must feel even worse knowing he has disappointed you.

21

Later I sit on my bed, a candle on the bureau. Even though the storm is over it might be hours before the power comes back. It's the first night in weeks that my room isn't hot and my fan isn't blowing. I hear the bullfrogs and crickets through my screen.

I can't wait for tomorrow. Sara and Brett are coming over. But first, I want to see Huey. I want to know what he thought about my pitching and the game.

There are footsteps on the stairs but it's too late to pretend I'm asleep.

"I came to say good night." Mom stands in the doorway, a candle in her hand. I mumble "Good night." We got through dinner without talking about anything.

She doesn't move and I glance at her. Her curly hair is

still wet from her shower. Her white cotton nightgown hangs loosely at her knees.

"It was nice to see you and Sara together." She pauses. "I said this at dinner, but I'm so proud of how you handled the season. You have courage and inner strength."

I roll my eyes. "Thanks."

"Listen." She walks to my window, glances out and turns. "Can we talk about all that's happened? I want to talk about this idea that you don't think I make mistakes."

"I don't want to talk about it!" I put my pillow over my face.

"I want to understand what you're feeling."

"Not now!"

All I see is blackness. Then I feel Mom's hand on my leg, her touch warm. She whispers "Good night" and when I think she's gone, I pull the pillow away. But then I feel so sad that she left me that I nearly yell for her to come back.

Later, when the power comes back on and my lights flood my room, I wake and sit up. I rub my eyes and look at my watch. 12:07. I turn out the lights. That's when I hear voices outside and the sound of a car idling. I look out my window.

Huey and Crystal are next to a taxi under the streetlight. The driver puts a duffel bag in his trunk and slams it. Huey is wearing his leather pants and a jacket. He leans into Crystal, as if to say something, but she pulls away and crosses her arms.

He's leaving! I want to call to him, but nothing comes

out of my mouth. Why is he going? Without Crystal? Without talking about the game?

Without saying goodbye to me?

I take out my screen, scoot across the roof, climb down the TV tower and run across the yard. Wet sand and pine needles stick to my feet. I reach Crystal just as the taxi climbs the hill. We watch until the brake lights redden the back of the taxi and it turns onto Lake Shore Drive and disappears.

"Where did he go?"

"Back to Hollywood." Crystal's voice is soft. "Or wherever."

I curl my toes underneath me and squeeze my fingers into fists. "Why?"

"It was time." Crystal shrugs.

Is this my fault? If I hadn't told Huey about Crystal's mom, maybe he would have stayed. Now he's gone and Crystal will be all alone again. All alone! "I told Huey about you running around in the snowstorm in your nightgown that night. I'm really sorry."

I feel sick to my stomach. I hold my breath and wait for her to yell at me.

"I know. He told me."

"It just slipped out. I wasn't planning on telling him."

Crystal chuckles. "You think he left because you told him about that night?"

"Well, yeah, I mean, I guess."

"Huey left because I asked him to go."

My mouth drops open. "You asked him to go? But I thought you two . . . that you and Huey . . . that maybe you were in love."

Crystal shakes her head. "Huey can't love anyone."

"Oh." I uncurl my fists. "Is he going back to his wife?"

"I don't think she wants him, either. He's a big baby, you know. He's almost forty and he can't do anything. He can't do laundry. He can't wash his cereal bowl. He sits on the couch and expects me to do everything. I don't need that. I don't need someone in front of the TV all day."

"But what about his writer's block?"

"Writer's block!" Crystal laughs. "The whole time he was here, he never tried to write. He's all washed up. He's a has-been. Plus, he's lazy."

He certainly *is* lazy. He never mowed Crystal's lawn. But he's good-looking, for an old guy, and smart. He gave good advice. He wrote great songs, even if that was a long time ago. And . . . something else, but I don't know what.

"He was interesting." And I really, really liked him. I really liked talking to him.

"Sure," she says. "And charming and cool and fun and sexy and a great kisser."

I glance at Crystal. Her lips seem extra thick and red. Her hair, pulled behind her ears, exposes her freckled cheeks. Crystal is six years older than David. But right now she seems so much older, and smarter, than either of us. Especially me.

She tilts her head. "You're going to miss him, huh?"

I nod.

"You don't know what happened that night of the snowstorm, do you?" I shake my head. "I asked your mom and the other Mother Hens not to tell anyone. Especially you. You had such a big mouth when you were a little kid."

Hot streaks race up my back. I'm about to complain when she goes on. "But you didn't tell anyone about Huey, did you? That, well, that was good."

I straighten. "Who are the Mother Hens?"

"Geneva, Carol, Pat. Your mom. That's what I call them."

Mrs. Minor, Mrs. Frazier, Mrs. Tulliver. "What do they have to do with this?"

Crystal looks up at the streetlight. Her voice is kind of hushed. "That night of the storm my mom and I had a big fight again. I went to my room to get away from her. Then hours later when I went to look for her, I found her in the car in the garage. I thought if I opened the garage door the cold air would get rid of the gas. But I was too late."

I feel little tingles inside my head, making me dizzy.

"The Mother Hens were always checking on me. After the funeral when my dad decided he wasn't going to stay and I sure wasn't going with him, they figured out how to help me keep the house. Your mom, she sure is one smart lady. She had it all worked out. They all helped me. Moneywise, if you know what I mean."

"Even Mrs. Minor?" I ask.

"Oh, yeah." Crystal chuckles. "She's basically a softy."

So Mrs. Adams didn't have a heart attack. Now I understand what Mom tried to tell me about Mrs. Adams's death. *Her heart finally gave out.* Her broken heart.

Something races across my back again. Crystal's mom didn't kill herself because they were fighting. Did she? I look at my dark house. My mom is in bed, dressed in her white nightgown and lying on her back. I know this.

202

"I better go."

"You're pretty lucky, you know. To have such a cool mom."

I glance at Crystal, the streetlight shining on her face. She doesn't seem like a maniac anymore. In fact, the only one who is acting like a maniac right now is me. Running after Huey. Misunderstanding everything.

"I gotta go." I sprint across Mrs. Minor's yard and into my own. The back door is unlocked, and I open the screen and start up the stairs. The hallway is dark. I feel along the wall until I'm standing in the doorway to Mom's room.

Streaks of moonlight shine through the window and fall across the bed. I watch her steady breathing, the way her hand drapes across her chest and how her hair scatters on the pillow. I remember what Mimi said one day when we'd just gotten here and I was sitting on Mom's lap, my ankles wrapped around her calves, our heads together. *You can't tell where one head of hair starts and the other ends.*

I was only five, but I remember leaving Germany. A woman Mom knew from the base drove us to the airport. The morning was rainy and cold, the car windows so smeared with fog and streaks of water that I couldn't see out. No one talked. Until finally that woman leaned over to Mom as we were getting out at the airport and said, "Lucky you."

For years afterward I thought she meant how lucky we were to go on a plane. But maybe she meant something else. Mom may have been the one to leave Dad. But if he could so easily give up the chance of ever seeing us again, then he couldn't have been that interested in us in the first place. And maybe everyone knew this but me.

I bite my lip. I've been so angry with her. But here she is. Sleeping. Breathing. Alive.

In the moonlight I watch her open her eyes and say, "Come here, Madison."

22

"You're awake." I step over a pile of newspapers and slip into bed next to her.

"I heard you on the roof," she says. I open my mouth but she puts her finger over my lips. "Then I got up and saw the taxi."

"Huey's gone." I close my eyes and breathe in the familiar smells of lemons and incense. When I was younger I always came in here in the middle of the night, snuggling and waiting to fall back asleep.

I feel a sob rise up in my throat. "I know how Mrs. Adams died."

I start crying although I'm not entirely sure why. I never really liked Mrs. Adams and up until tonight I didn't much like Crystal, either. But it's all so sad and Crystal is so brave. And I don't want anything to ever, ever happen to my mom.

"Oh, honey." She slides her arm under my shoulder and pulls me toward her. I stiffen but then relax and settle into her arms.

"Why?" I ask.

"She was so unhappy. And so, so sick."

"But Crystal said they'd had a fight. Then she found her."

Mom pushes my hair, one curl at a time, from my face and wipes away the tears. "Mrs. Adams had a sickness. A mental illness. She was so unhappy that she couldn't see anything else but that."

"Crystal didn't make her do it?"

Mom leans up on her elbow. I see her profile in the moonlight, the lines in the corners of her eyes, the sharpness of her cheekbones, the curls that fall across her face.

"Oh, no. This had nothing to do with Crystal. It's unfortunate that they had a fight. But Crystal knows it wasn't her fault. Her mother was very sick. People tried to help her. At one point she went away to a hospital for a while but nothing helped."

Mom lies down and we're quiet. Maybe no one could do anything for Mrs. Adams, but my mom did something for Crystal. "Crystal calls you and the neighbors Mother Hens," I say.

"I know."

"You helped her stay in the house. That's why you kept bugging her about going to night classes. Right? You were trying to help her."

Mom is quiet for a moment. "Someone had to look out for her. As women, we have a responsibility to take care of each other."

I cringe, but only for a second. "Why didn't you ever tell me this?"

"Crystal asked me not to tell anyone."

I breathe in. "Crystal told Huey to leave. She didn't want him around anymore."

"Ah."

"I'm really going to miss him. It was so easy to talk to him." I wait for her to say something, but she doesn't. "He's married but he and his wife don't live together. Do you think he'll go back home? But Crystal said his wife probably doesn't want him, either."

"Mmm."

"She said Huey couldn't love anyone. But she also said he was fun to be with. And a good kisser. So I guess she wasn't in love with him after all."

"Apparently not."

We're quiet again. Then I know what I really want to talk about. "Is this how you felt about Dad?" I hold my breath.

"Well, I certainly loved kissing him. Your dad could be so passionate and exciting. But I wanted a best friend *and* someone who made me feel good inside *and* someone who wanted to be with us, be a family man. He couldn't be all of those things."

I remember how nice it felt when Tommy tickled my hand. But it wasn't much fun being with him. And my reasons for liking him were pretty lame.

I close my eyes. Maybe someday I'll have a boyfriend who is my best friend *and* who makes me feel good inside.

I open my eyes and stare at the streaks of moonlight across the bed. Tomorrow the newspaper will have a write-up about the game and there'll be something on TV, too. People will talk about how I struck out Billy. Then in my mind I see Mom, her hands on her cheeks, as I was pitching.

"Were you nervous, watching me pitch tonight?"

"I was extremely nervous, every time you pitched. It was excruciating, actually."

"Really? Why?"

"Because I love you and don't want you to be hurt or unhappy. And I worried about all that pressure on you."

"I don't think Billy's dad felt very worried about him."

My mom tightens her grip around my shoulder.

"David thinks I should play middle league next year."

"Oh? What do you think?"

"I don't know. I mean, I'll miss pitching and stuff. But I won't miss . . ."

I stop.

"Let's see," Mom says. "You won't miss the catcalls from the crowd and the anxiety over being the only girl and the articles in the newspaper and the attention."

"That's right."

"I sure won't miss that part of it, either."

"You won't?"

"No."

We're quiet for a moment.

"I've been thinking a lot about our conversation

208

yesterday," she says. "I think I've done you a disservice by not letting you see mistakes I've made. I guess I wanted to protect you and help you feel safe."

"Can we talk about this tomorrow?"

She squeezes me.

I settle back against her and close my eyes again. I feel myself dozing, then floating, and I imagine I'm on the lake, the waves gently pushing me forward and backward and around. And the sun is hot but the humidity is gone, just the way it's supposed to be later today, when Sara and Brett come over.

It's so strange how things have worked out. David wants to be a baseball player but he's not good enough. I'm good enough but I don't want it. I was envious because Billy had his dad as a coach, when all along Mr. Weeks and David were perfectly good coaches, especially David. I thought I wanted Tommy as my boyfriend.

Maybe Huey was right after all. Maybe we always want what we don't have.

I wonder if I'll wake up and still be bugged by Mom's clothes and the things she says and does.

I pull a bunch of hair across my lips and chew on it. It's full and thick and smells like lemons. When I realize that this is Mom's hair, not my own, I wrap it around my chin and leave it there.

And then I close my eyes and go to sleep.

Acknowledgments

Many thanks to my editor, Wendy Lamb, and assistant editor Caroline Meckler for encouraging me to dig deeper. To my agent, Amy Jameson, who sent me back to the drawing board. To my readers, Alison Dinsmore, Bryn Wood, Regina Assetta, Jennifer Christie, Christina Solazzo, Alison Weiss, my critique group and mostly and especially Kathy Read (and Sam, too). To Gary Day, who still holds a state pitching record. Lots of love and thanks to David, Elizabeth, Emma and Dylan.

About the Author

KAREN DAY grew up in Indiana and now lives in Newton, Massachusetts, with her husband and their three children. Her love of reading and writing has taken her through careers in journalism and teaching. Her first novel for children was *Tall Tales*, also published by Wendy Lamb Books. You can visit Karen at www.klday.com.